THE DEVIL'S SOCIETY

HOMECOMING

KINSLEY KINCAID

Paperback ISBN - 978-1-0688482-1-6

eBook ISBN - 978-1-0688482-0-9

Editing: Rumi Khan

Proofreading: Daisie Mae & Lori Rivera

Cover Design: Occult Goddess

***Revised October 2024 – Formally part of The Exodus Series**

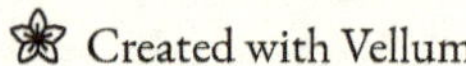 Created with Vellum

NOTE FROM THE AUTHOR

Please be aware this book contains many **dark themes** and subjects that may be uncomfortable/unsuitable for some readers. This book contains **heavy themes** throughout. Please keep this in mind when entering Homecoming. Content warnings are listed on authors' social pages & website.

This book and its contents are entirely a work of fiction. Any resemblance or similarities to names, characters, organizations, places, events, incidents, or real people are entirely coincidental or used fictitiously.

If you find any genuine errors, please reach out to the author directly to correct it. Thank you.

This book is intended for 18+ only.

PLAYLIST

Welcome - Homecoming Live - Beyonce
n/A - Bring Me The Horizon
Demons - Imagine Dragons
Faded - Alan Walker
Lonely Road - mgk, Jelly Roll
The Monster - Eminem, Rihanna
ANGELS & DEMONS - jxdn
All My Life - Falling in Reverse, Jelly Roll
willow - Taylor Swift
Who's Afraid of Little Old Me? - Taylor Swift
Watch The World Burn - Falling in Reverse
Down with the Sickness - Disturbed
Coward - iamjakehill
Tear You Apart - She Wants Revenge
I Don't Care (with Justin Bieber) - Ed Sheeran
DArkSide - Bring Me The Horizon
Psychopath Killer - Slaughterhouse, Yelawolf, Eminem
Violence - Blink-182
Dress - Taylor Swift

Lollipop - Lil Wayne, Static Major
Watermelon Sugar - Harry Styles
VVV - HE'S BACK - mikeeysmind, Sanikwave
Psycho Killer - Talking Heads

Spotify Playlist

SPECIAL NOTE

Some references made are from *Sinner*, which is Elijah's origin story.

Reading Order of Elijah's Duet

Haunted by the Devil
Homecoming
Sinner; Before Rain - Prequel*

*Can be read before, between or after the duet.

If you thought Haunted was fucked. You haven't seen shit yet, my little bats.

"Do it. Fucking coward."

This dumb bitch is on my last nerve.

Declining her birthright.

She was given a choice. She didn't pick the right one.

Now it's time for her to face the consequences. She was warned.

Music is pounding. The floor of the second-story balcony vibrates beneath our feet.

"Jump!"

A whimper leaves her mouth, her body shaking with fear. Fear which she put inside of herself. It didn't have to be this way.

Stepping behind her, his mouth grazes her ear as a harsh whisper leaves his lips. "No one will miss you anyways."

A loud scream leaves her.

Feet that were balancing on the wooden banister only moments ago are now floating in the air as she jumps.

The red fabric hanging from the ceiling dances. My

eyes are captivated by it. Then a loud snap catches my attention.

"Fucking beautiful, isn't it?"

CHAPTER 1

ELIJAH

"Little bat, wake up. We are home."

Rain's been asleep since we landed. Her head rests on my lap with her legs curled into her body. She is wearing black leggings, one of my black hoodies, and white high-tops. My fingers have been mindlessly playing with her dark hair the entire time as I dick around on my phone.

We were picked up from the private airstrip by one of my dad's drivers in a blacked-out SUV.

It's been ten fucking years since I have been back to Bozeman, Montana.

I'm impartial about being back.

I've never tried to run and hide from it, my responsibilities. By going to Blackwood all those years ago with my mom and that charismatic cunt, it gave me an opportunity to experience life outside of here, which I can apply now that I am back.

Bozeman, and what's to come next have always been in the cards for me.

These fuckers won't know what hit them, so many new people to play with.

A smirk forms on my face, another memory flashing before me. It's the old shed out back at my dad's place, where I learned the fundamentals. The smell of blood as it coats my fingers, pushing his eyes as hard as I can into the backs of his eye sockets.

The screams were a symphony.

My other hand rubs the hard wood of my bat, which is resting between my feet and leaning against the door. "We will celebrate at our homecoming tomorrow."

Looking out the tinted window, the private road which is home to my house and my dad's is decorated with large green spruce trees, the grass browning as fall will soon become winter. It's October.

The road is able to remain private as it's blocked by a gate which only me, my dad, and a few staff members have access to entering. The vehicle turns into my driveway, while Dad's is across the street.

Security has been embedded into me since I can remember.

"Rain, if you don't wake up, I have no problem

punishing you later." My voice is low so the driver doesn't hear. He can mind his own fucking business.

Her body stretches out, a moan of discontent escaping her mouth as she whines. "If you even try, I'll use my choke pear on you."

A loud chuckle leaves my lips.

This fucking girl.

Rain had been looking up different torture techniques when she discovered the choke pear, which happened to be at the same time I was tattooing my teeth marks onto her ass. She's been obsessed with it ever since. I ordered one for our place in Blackwood, which she proudly displays on her nightstand. A second one was ordered for here as soon as I got the call from Dad. It's a surprise for my little bat, to make her feel more at home. Even though it's due to arrive today, I'll have Rogers keep it hidden until tomorrow.

For lack of a better word, he is like our property manager. Anything and everything we need, he is the man to procure it for us.

For Rain, this trip was sudden; for me, it's been years in the making.

Blackwood will be where we go to get away, spend the summers, and visit her mom.

This place, Bozeman, is her new home. I just haven't broken the news to her yet.

The SUV comes to a stop outside the oversized dark wood front door, which is enclosed by a stone archway.

The rest of the exterior is decorated with granite rock and large windows on the single-story home. A four-car garage is on the far side of the house. Unlike Blackwood, this garage only holds cars.

Like the private road, the entire property is surrounded by a forest of trees. The backyard is also home to a pool and hot tub, along with an outdoor patio space and kitchen.

My dad started building this place for me when I was seventeen, ensuring it would be ready for when I needed to return. He would send me progress reports and I would provide feedback on what I needed. A lot of it I left up to him, with the exception of a few sacred places.

Such as one of the two basements which sits under the house.

Rain sits up, the side of her face flushed from resting on my legs. She looks over to me, still tired. "How long did you say we would be here for?"

Gripping my bat, I open the car door and begin to step out as I respond, "I didn't."

It's later in the evening, the sun has already started to set and the air is cold and crisp. Mountains surround us behind the trees, the clouds hang low and threaten snow upon us at any moment. Soon a sea of tourists will invade for the winter ski season.

But first, a tradition which is generations old must occur. Something that only happens every five years. Locals all know it's coming, they leave or stay inside. Preparation begins the day following the last one.

Hell Fire Night.

Tourists who come early catch on quickly when things begin to shut down early for the night. The town goes quiet as we come out to play.

"When do we meet your dad?"

Turning around, I take another deep breath in.

To most, the smell of this place calms them, connects them with nature. To me, it's calming but for completely different reasons. It connects me to death.

This is where I learned to embrace myself.

Since that day at the dinner table when I was five, sitting with my dad's "friends", who I now know are much more than that, it's been death.

I will always remember when Dad pulled me aside in his office, how his one friend said I would be useful.

That's when it began—no longer having to keep my demons at bay.

My dad gave me permission to be my fucking self.

Keeping my expression neutral, I reply, "Soon. If not tonight, definitely tomorrow."

She nods her head, accepting my short answers as she slides to exit on my side of the car.

Joining me outside, her eyes take it all in as her jaw drops. "This place is incredible, E."

Grabbing her at the waist, I pull her close against me and whisper in her ear, "You haven't seen the best of it yet, little bat."

Reaching up, her tiny fingers trace the lines of my ink

that decorate my face. She loves doing this. "Then show me."

Not taking my eyes off her hazel ones that I'll forever be captivated by. "Gladly."

Taking her hand in mine, I lead her up a stone step. It only takes a couple more steps as we reach the front door. Turning the iron handle, the latch clicks as I push it open. It's unlocked, so I suspect Rogers left it that way on purpose.

Which fucking annoys me, and he knows it.

A loud gasp comes from behind me as we walk in.

The space is all open, large dark wood beams running across the white ceiling. A tall, dark stone, wood fireplace reaches from the wood floor to the tallest peak of the ceiling. A nook is carved out within where a large television is mounted, with built-in bookshelves lining both sides. A large glass coffee table and two oversized cream couches finish the area off.

Large windows line the back wall, which are tinted and overlook the patio and outdoor space that houses a kitchen, hot tub, pool which is covered until next summer, and acres of green space and forest.

Iron chandeliers hang from the ceiling and a dining space is off to one side by the living room, with the kitchen and oversized island on the other. A hallway off the kitchen leads to the master wing. An additional hallway just off the entrance leads to the guest rooms and garage.

"E, this place is incredible. You can see the mountains from here!" Rain shakes my hand with excitement.

Embracing her into another hug and resting my chin on the top of her head, I picture her naked in my basement and coated in blood. My cock gets hard, pushing against my jeans. "I still have so much to show you, little bat."

CHAPTER 2

ELIJAH

Thankfully, this place is stocked with everything we need. Tonight we can relax before the chaos begins tomorrow.

My skin itches with need. It's been a couple months since everything went down in Blackwood and I need this release.

As Rain unpacks in her walk-in closet—I have my own—she shouts, "Why did I even bring a suitcase? This closet is completely full!"

I don't respond.

"Eventually you will have to tell me why we are here and what the fuck is going on."

There she is.

Tired Rain is far too sweet, which is fine once in a while, but I prefer her like this. No bullshit, speaks her mind, my little bat.

As she appears in the entrance way with her arms crossed and eyebrows raised, my phone vibrates in my pant pocket while I am sitting in the lounge chair next to the large window in the bedroom. Pulling it out, I see it's a text from my dad saying he will be over later tonight.

Placing the phone down on the table next to me, I stand up, walking over to Rain.

Looking down at her, she doesn't budge, her face still annoyed with her arms crossed over her chest.

Roughly, I brush my thumb across her lips. "On your knees. Your filthy mouth needs to be filled."

The corner of her lip tries to smirk but she stops it. Not wanting to show the effect this has on her. If there is one thing I know, my little bat loves sucking my cock, and she is going to fucking do it like a champ whether she wants to or not right now.

"My dad's coming tonight, so you will get your answers then. But right now, I will be coming down your throat. Now, get on your fucking knees," my voice rasps, mixed with authority and need.

She challenges me, keeping eye contact and raising her brow. It's all part of our little game with one another.

"I'll give you a treat after, don't worry, little bat."

This has piqued her interest. Rain's eyes sparkle at the new incentive. Biting her lip, she slowly begins to kneel down before me. Her eyes never leave mine, they become more dilated with each second. As her fingers touch my button and zipper, my cock becomes rock hard, waiting to come out and play.

Popping the button quickly, she makes sure to do my zipper slowly. It takes every ounce of self-restraint to not do it for her and shove my cock into the back of her throat. But I know what she's doing. Punishing me for not giving her any information about why we are really here.

Sometimes it's easier to see it than hear it.

And if I were to explain that I am also from a corrupt family, who allowed me to embrace my needs, who has had control over the local government and has been the force behind many crime organizations in the area for generations, I'm not sure she would believe me.

Typically, I couldn't give a fuck if someone believes me or not.

But with her, everything is different.

Chilled hands on my cock send a shiver up my spine. My eyes are still on her, but her eyes are now focused elsewhere.

Licking her lips, her tongue brushes my tip and laps my piercing, toying with me.

A low growl leaves me. "Suck."

Her lips slide slowly as her tongue continues to tease me, licking the underside as she begins to take me all the way to the back of her mouth.

Reaching down, I gather her loose, dark long hair into my hands, holding it up for her at the back of her head.

"Such a good girl for me, little bat."

My eyes hood as I watch her, and her lips plump as

they wrap around me. I can feel my piercing rub against her throat as she takes me deep. Gagging briefly, some drool drips from her bottom lip onto her chin. Unable to help myself, I take control. The sight of her like this always sends me into a frenzy.

With my hands still tangled in her hair, I hold her head as I begin to rapidly thrust myself into her mouth. Her teeth graze me. She has the power here, not me. One move is all it takes for her to be biting down on me, with blood from my cock spilling out of her mouth with that devious look in her eye, fuck me. The tease is thrilling and she fucking knows it.

Continuing my assault on her mouth, her hands grip my thighs and a stream of tears fall from her eyes.

"I'm almost there, little bat. You are so fucking beautiful like this."

Looking up at me, Rain lifts her brow slightly, as if to say, *is that all you got?* Oh, my sweet little bat, as you fucking wish.

The entire length of my cock disappears. My head is well down her throat and I don't let up, knowing she will be gasping for air any moment now.

As she tries to breathe, her throat contracts around me, which reminds me of how her pussy feels as it milks me dry.

My balls tighten as my heart races, beating against my chest as that familiar feeling takes over. Ropes of warm come begin to coat her throat as she continues to milk me, searching for any bit of air she can get.

Tears continue to stream down her once pale skin, now a beautiful shade of red. Long strings of drool hang from her mouth and chin as I work myself through my release.

"You are so fucking perfect. And all fucking mine. MINE!" I shout as the final bit of release leaves me.

As my movements slow down, I begin to pull out of her, giving her the oxygen her body craves. Breathing through her nose, she releases her hands from my thighs as I pull completely out of her. Rain's hands go to the ground in front of her as she takes deep gasps of air. Her face is blotchy and a mix of my cum and her saliva coats her lips, leaving them glistening.

Tucking myself back in and pulling up my pants, I give her another minute before reaching my hand out to her.

Tiny fingers touch my palm and wrapping my large fingers over hers, I pull her up to her fuzzy sock-clad feet and kiss her deep.

The taste of my cum touches my taste buds as our tongues dance together, but I don't fucking care. Devouring her, we go from dancing to battling for dominance. My teeth nip her lip as a tiny moan escapes her.

Rain pulls back, causing us to disconnect, and I hate it. Nostrils flare as I look down at her, smirking.

"I will get you back for that," she promises. And I don't doubt it. I hope she does, and it better fucking hurt.

Wiping her chin with my thumb, I place it in my mouth and suck.

Her eyes look at me curiously. "So, are you going to show me or what?"

"Yeah." Grabbing her hand, I lace our fingers together. "Come with me."

Pulling her behind me, we walk quickly through the house. No telling when my dad will arrive, but I want to show her this. She fucking deserves to see this.

Cutting through the living space and past the dining table, we walk through the guest side of the house. A few doors line either side, at the end of the hallway is a large window which is as wide and high as the wall it sits in.

It's dark now, with only a sliver of moonlight sneaking in.

On the left side of the hallway, there is a dark wooden door like the rest, or so it would seem. Next to it is a scanner, which is programmed with my thumbprint. Placing it over the scanner, the device comes to life and a red light beams under the pad of my thumb, then a green light follows, unlocking the secured door. You hear the click of the latch releasing before I reach out with my free hand and turn the brass knob, opening the heavy door. It is lined with wood to appear normal, but underneath it is thick steel to keep out any unwanted guests.

Rain's fingers squeeze mine tighter. "E, what's down there?" she asks skeptically.

Flicking the switch, bright fluorescent lights turn on, each one hanging by electrical cords that hide into the ceiling and hover over the long staircase leading to the basement.

The walls are white, which goes with the white heated tile stairs.

"Follow me. And close the door behind you."

I let go of her hand. The staircase is narrow, and my boots pound against each step as I make my way down. As I reach the bottom, I flip another switch, which lights up the entire space. The floor is the same white tile, that also lines the walls.

Makes it easier to clean.

The space is one thousand square feet, a fraction of the size of my place. When my dad started building this place for me, he put this space in specifically for me and my needs. It is directly under the garage, which can be accessed via another staircase on the other side of the room. This way nothing tracks inside my house. The cleanup crew, when needed, comes in and out through the garage entrance, along with my playthings, victims some may say.

It can easily fit two people comfortably tied up on a chair or table—or hanging with their limbs tied to the ceiling, depending on my mood.

Like Blackwood, cabinets line the area which home my preferred tools. A couple drains are on the floor and a sink is connected. Right now, as it's not in use, two embalming tables are laid out in the middle. Hanging from all four corners are restraints, each equipped with a rack. When activated, they will pull at the tied-up limbs, stretching them out until I either stop it or they pop out of their sockets and tear off the bodies.

It's something I had at my dad's place and fucking loved. I needed it here.

When not in use, they can be raised to the ceiling, so they are out of the way for other fun activities.

A television hangs in one of the corners, CCTV for my security outside. Should someone come by while I am busy, I can see who it is and decide if they are worth stopping my fun for.

This space has yet to be used, and I am itching to break it in. The part of my brain which homes urges and desires, the limbic system, is on fire with need.

I can fucking taste it in my mouth, smell the copper in my nose, and see the pathetic fucker laying lifelessly on the table as their blood drains out of them.

Tomorrow.

I'll feel fully satisfied again—tomorrow.

Turning around, I look at Rain. Her mouth is closed but her eyes are wide open.

"What do you think?"

Stepping forward, she brushes her hand against the stainless-steel table, taking it all in.

A small whisper leaves her mouth, "It's perfect."

Her body jumps as a loud buzz goes off in the quiet space. "What was that?"

Walking over to one of the cabinets, I find the television remote and turn it on.

The doorbell.

Staring back at us is an older man with slightly slicked-back salt-and-pepper hair, circle wire-framed eyeglasses, wearing a navy-blue suit and a white dress shirt with no tie. A white pocket square sticks out of his breast pocket, and his facial features strongly resemble mine: a strong jawline, thick brows, and the same impatient look I get when I am kept waiting.

"You're about to get all the answers to your questions, little bat. Dad's here."

CHAPTER 3

RAIN

"Nathaniel Sinclair."

Elijah greets his dad as he opens the large front door. He is standing under the overhead porch lighting, his features familiar but more posh, upper-class, and less rugged than the ones I'm used to.

I wonder how similar they really are?

Standing off to the side, I'm unsure of how this reunion will go. E has never been open about his family life outside of his mom and my dad. I've known him to text his dad, he has never said a bad thing about him truthfully, but I have no idea if they are close or what terms they were on when E left Montana.

His dad's hands are in his trouser pockets, wearing a navy-blue suit, and a white shirt with dark brown dress shoes, he raises his brow at Elijah. "Something's changed, but I can't quite put my finger on it. New piercing?"

Elijah blows out a breath of annoyance, which I am sure is accompanied with an eye roll. I begin to feel a smirk forming on my face, I've never seen anyone joke with E before. I like it.

"I'm just messin' with you, kid. It suits you. It's... you." His dad briefly looks my way and winks before focusing back on E.

He's talking about the face tattoo.

"Are you going to invite me in? And who is this?" He nods his head toward me.

Elijah stands back, bringing the door fully open, and extending his arm. "Please, come in."

As his dad walks in, E closes the door behind him.

Reaching a hand out to me, he says, "Nate, you can call me Nate."

Meeting him in the middle, I awkwardly shake it. "Rain. Rain Sinclair."

I don't know why I said that.

Nate doesn't look away, still shaking my hand while looking like he is deep in thought.

"Interesting, very interesting."

I swallow a giant lump down my throat. What does he mean, interesting?

"Isn't it?" E is quick to jump in.

Nate lets go of my hand and focuses back on his son. All I can focus on is this older version of my Elijah before us. Ink decorates his exposed skin, faded black and gray can be seen from his neck to his hands and fingers. The smell of vanilla and sandalwood tickles my senses.

Once I return my focus, the three of us walk toward the couches in the living room in awkward silence, or at least it is awkward for me. Our shoes against the hardwood are the only sounds filling the void.

I sit down in the lone lounge chair as E and his dad take a couch each. Both sitting on the ends closest to each other, they both extend their long legs and cross them at the ankles. The heels of their feet rest only a few inches from one another.

"It's surreal having you back. I always knew this day would come, but now that it's here I'm not sure I believe it yet." Nate's head is resting against the back of the couch as he looks up at the ceiling, rubbing his face.

Elijah doesn't immediately respond, his eyes are still taking everything in. His mind is racing, trying to figure out how to respond and handle this situation. It's unfamiliar to him. He is trying to sort out how to feel, *if* he feels.

His dad's head turns slightly to look at him, though he doesn't force anything. He lets his son take the time he needs.

"Are you mad about Mom? What I did, what I forced her to do?"

I'm shocked by the question.

Elijah does things because he wants to, because he needs to.

He doesn't show remorse or ask for approval after the fact. I remain silent, observing the interaction.

Nate sits up, resting his elbows on his thighs and leaning forward. His head shakes as he focuses on a spot in front of him. "No. I would never be mad at you for being yourself and doing what you need to do."

"Good. Because I don't feel bad about it. I put up with her and that dumb fuck for ten years too long. She deserved everything she got. And I would do it over and over again," Elijah says casually in response.

"Not that you need to hear this. You did the right thing."

Nate's confession of support shocks me.

These two have a bond I can't yet describe, but it's unique and supportive. Nate is someone Elijah trusts.

"You're right, I don't. But... Thank you. The shit the two of them did to Rain. The smile on my face as she stepped back into the fire." E closes his eyes and inhales. "I can still smell her burning skin in that cave. The sound of her pathetic screams." His thumbs itch the side of his fingers, which his dad picks up on.

As E opens his eyes, a devious glint appears. One I haven't seen in months. One that I have fucking missed, to be honest. It was starting to worry me. How long could he go without hurting? What happens if he can't keep it contained?

As E goes to reach for his bat, out of habit—he does that sometimes even if it's not next to him—his hand falls into the air.

Nate grins, still leaning forward and now looking at me. "I got him that bat when he was five. At the time, I didn't understand the significance behind him asking for it. It's been attached to him since and now it's a part of him. An extension of himself."

"And he's magnificent with it," I proudly respond. My body relaxes more into the chair. Seeing how they are together, it's comforting.

"That he is."

E interrupts, impatient, still itching at his hand, "Are you going to continue to talk about me like I'm not here?"

Nate changes the subject, "What's with the twitching fingers?"

You could hear a pin drop, the room goes absolutely silent. E doesn't respond.

"How long?"

Elijah looks away from us, mumbling under his breath, "Two months."

"I see."

His dad's facial expression remains neutral, it makes him incredibly hard to read. He can shut off his emotions as easily as his son.

Blowing out a deep breath, his head turns to Elijah, who is still not looking at us. "We've been saving them all for tomorrow. I don't even have anyone I could give you tonight. I'm sorry, son."

You can tell he means it. As unreadable as his face is, his voice is sympathetic to his son's predicament.

This is a man who truly loves his son. I can feel it, I can see it, it's so strong. It reminds me of my mom.

Turning his head back to us, his brow furrows, eyes squinting, and I can tell he is agitated. I'm sure this is a lot coming back here, plus knowing he can't release his demons until tomorrow, I don't blame him. "Is the shed still out back at your place?"

"It is," his dad responds curiously while gingerly nodding his head.

"Good, I want to show her everything. I'll bring her by tomorrow, before Hell Fire Night."

I'm quick to interrupt. "What is Hell Fire Night?"

Nate smirks, questioning his son, "You haven't told her why you both are here?"

E doesn't respond, letting his dad continue, "It happens every five years and always lands on the tenth day of the tenth month at ten p.m. on the fifth year. It is a rite of passage for some, like Elijah. This is his birthright. Others are forced to make a decision. The wrong choice could land them a grave deep in the woods."

I sit with what he has just said. "Like an initiation?" I question as I am trying to understand.

"Sort of. I'll let him explain it in more detail to you. Because this should really be coming from him since he brought you in."

Looking over at E, he nods, blowing out another breath of exhaustion. "I will."

As his dad stands, E follows, already anticipating the next move.

Nate looks at his watch. "I best go. Your masks are almost ready, I'll leave them with Rogers. Grab them when you're done." Then he looks toward me. "Rain, it was a pleasure meeting you."

I smile genuinely back at him and remain sitting, allowing E and his dad to have a moment as they both walk to the door.

A few words are spoken, but I can't quite make them out.

As the front door opens, Nate's hand grips his son's shoulder, squeezing it a couple times before letting go and leaving.

As E closes the door behind his dad, he turns around to look at me. "He knew I changed your name to Sinclair. Don't let him fool you, he knows more than most. But..." He pauses, deep in thought. "You can always trust him. If anything ever happens to me, you go to him. He will help you. Do you understand me?"

Nodding my head, I take it all in.

Everything is starting to hit me at once.

Birthright, generational, saving *them* for tomorrow?

I have gone from one hell to another. But in this hell, it appears we may be the ones in control.

CHAPTER 4

RAIN

E is on edge. He hasn't slept.

He is acting like a drug addict going through withdrawals, but knowing his next hit is only hours away, there is an added intensity to his insanity.

I still don't completely understand everything. His family is deeply involved in something bigger than my brain can comprehend at the moment.

Wandering around the house, I find myself in the guest wing as my hand mindlessly plays with my black leather collar decorated with rose gold accents which encompasses his vial of blood, his soul, in the center.

Passing the secure door, I pause. Turning slowly I face it, placing my hand on the door, and a chill runs up my spine. It doesn't make sense.

E is still in the backyard.

He has been out there since before I woke up. When making my morning coffee, I watched him through the massive back windows. Sitting on the patio furniture, his back to me, spinning his bat mindlessly next to him on the patio stones with his tattooed fingers.

The clouds were overcast, his breath floated in the air, and it made me wonder, how the fuck am I supposed to get used to this weather?

As I stood and watched him from the kitchen island, he threw his head back at one point and yelled into the morning sky. It's possible he felt me watching. But I doubt it. At that moment, he was the most vulnerable I had ever seen. This is completely out of character for him. The restraint he is showing is mind-blowing, the fact that he hasn't just said *fuck it* and gone out to satisfy his cravings shows that deep down, even if he can't express it or properly articulate it, he does have some self-restraint against the voices, the demons that whisper *kill, kill, kill.*

It's midday, and he still hasn't come in.

I've gotten ready in a pair of oversized sweats and a hoodie. I know we have to go to his dad's before this evening begins. Even when dressed warmly, the chill from touching the door lingers up my spine.

As I remove my hand, I take a deep breath in and decide I have to get him. I need to help keep his mind busy. Turning around, the eerie feeling remains, while a familiar one is added.

He is here.

My eyes look to the end of the long hall, and E is looking back at me from through the large window. Half of his tattooed face is covered with a shadow, his expression stone. Resting over his shoulder is his wooden bat. His outfit matches mine, all black. With a slight tilt of his head, I know, he tells me it's time to go.

My feet pad across the hardwood as I find my shoes by the front entrance. Quickly, I slide them on and rush out the front door. I am eager to learn more.

A cool breeze tickles my cheeks. My lungs cough, adjusting to the dry, cool air.

Rubbing my hands together, my eyes wander the property, looking for him.

Where did he go?

Stepping down the large step, I shove my hands in my pockets and begin walking up the long stone driveway. It's unlikely he has made it this far, but I don't know where else to go. My mind races, I still feel connected to him like on that very first day while I was working at the bar, but I also feel very uneasy. He is isolating. And I don't know how to fucking help him.

Perhaps the feeling of being useless is what is driving it. I am uncomfortable because I am unable to help him, when it's all I want to be able to do. It hurts my soul knowing he is hurting. He would end anyone and anything in his path to help me. And I am here, walking up a driveway racking my goddamn brain, trying not to feel bad when this isn't about me.

Spiraling.

Tiny pebbles crack under my feet as I continue to walk up the driveway.

I feel *him*.

A loud whistle behind me catches my attention, causing me to stop in my tracks. Turning my head, his beautiful eyes catch my attention first. The blue with the specks of brown thrive here. They were never this vibrant in North Carolina. This is where he is meant to be.

Smiling at the sight before me, E is driving a black-on-black golf cart in my direction .

"We aren't walking," is all he says as he stops next to me.

Once I am seated next to him, his foot presses down on the gas. His bat rests between us and rolls slightly at the acceleration. His fingers are holding the steering wheel tightly, knuckles white, as he tries to fight the twitching, the anxiety. His breathing is heavy.

Reaching my hand out, I place it on his thigh. His muscles contract under my soft touch while his teeth grind, my poor sweet boy.

With squinted eyes, he drives us up his long drive, across the private road, and down his dad's driveway.

Like Elijah's, trees surround the home, privacy is very important to this family, so I am learning. The home is immaculate. Two-story log home with accents of rock. Easily double the size of E's place. It even has two front entrances on either side. A large fountain is in the middle, which we circle as E parks to the closer of the two front doors. Putting it in park, then switching the golf cart off, he grabs his bat and gets out. My hand breaks contact and is already missing his warmth.

Getting out, I silently follow his lead.

I always promised I would follow him without question in this area, and it is a promise I intend to keep, even if my soul is screaming from watching him suffer.

With his hood covering his head, short pieces of his dark hair stick out.

He is gorgeous.

"I know you're checking me out." Turning his head to me, he winks before carrying on forward. It's the first bit of joy I have seen from him in days.

A piece of him is still inside this shell of a man, trying to show me it's okay.

Instead of going inside, he starts to walk around the house—it's a compound, really. This property is insane and slightly overwhelming.

Cameras can be seen around the home and hiding in the trees as I take everything in. Steel shutters cover the second-story windows, which is unique. Iron fencing appears, not just posts but entire solid pieces. E puts his thumb up against one part and the buzzing of the gate begins before clicking open. Pushing the gate open, he exposes the backyard, which is surrounded by dense forest. Walking up the side of the house, I continue to follow as my curious eyes take everything in.

A beautiful view of the mountains keeps my attention, some peaks are already decorated in white snow.

Without noticing, Elijah has stopped and the side of

my face meets the soft fabric of his hoodie. My feet briefly try to lose their balance by stumbling backward, which I try to prevent by gripping onto the back of him. Helping, he leans forward slightly.

A hiss leaves his mouth, my face scrunches in confusion. *Did I hurt him?*

"Are you okay?"

He doesn't respond with words, only a nod of his head.

As I let go of his hoodie, I find his free hand and interlace my fingers with his. Looking up at him, his teeth are biting on his lip ring, playing with it absent-mindedly.

Anxiety.

Hesitantly, I ask, "How can I help?" I hate feeling helpless with him. He does so much for me, protects and takes care of me. I need to help him in his time of need now.

"You can't."

He is short in his response. Nothing taken personally, I can only imagine how it must feel being in his head right now. Battling the demons and holding them off, it must be exhausting.

At the same time, I didn't realize until now, how much not killing would hurt him. He has been accustomed to acting on his urges since he was a child. What was I thinking? Of course he would get an itch, which he hasn't scratched in months.

As we step farther into the large backyard, there is an

old building, possibly the shed I heard him reference yesterday with his dad. But I can't be sure. He will tell me once he is ready.

E squeezes my hand, and the corner of my lip rises.

He is still in there.

Leading us closer to the tree line, I continue to look around. The backyard is pretty bare with the exception of the large patio at the back of the house, which is a giant outdoor living space, and the shed.

As we stop on the lawn, standing side by side before the forest of trees, I look deep within. It doesn't look as full as they would in North Carolina. Leaves fallen, branches bare with multiple tones of brown are before me. Some green spruce trees are in the mix, giving us that pop of color that I am so familiar with.

A breeze blows past, making the tip of my nose cold and starting to run as I sniffle it back.

"This is a graveyard." As he speaks, his arm lifts, pointing to the woods with his bat.

My eyes squint, I don't see any headstones.

"More bodies are buried here than you can even fucking imagine. Whatever number you are thinking, at least double it. Triple it, even. The graves are generations old."

Fuck me.

My eyes widen, taking it in.

"When I was five, I was introduced to the lifestyle. One question at dinner with my dad and his friends about killing a person, turned into my tendencies being nurtured. My dad never got mad. He only asked how he could help. He then set me up with a mentor to hone my craft. He never made me feel different or fucked in the head."

E points his bat in another direction beside me, but farther up the property. "That's the shed."

Just as I suspected.

"At the time, I didn't realize that dinner was full of powerful people who also supported my learnings. Before my question, they were just my dad's friends who came over often. But then everything changed because of one fucking question. *What is the best way to kill someone?* Maybe things do happen for a reason, I don't fucking know. But it seems to have all worked out."

I want to look at him, but I worry he will stop sharing if I do, so I continue looking forward.

He lowers his bat next to him again and continues, "As years went on, I went from learning the fundamentals at five—torture, dismemberment, and disposing. To kidnapping and killing by the age of ten, when I left here for Blackwood. My mentor always told me, '*You can't kill if you don't know how to handle the bodies after. Usually there is a cleanup crew, but not in all cases. You have to fucking know how to cover your tracks.*' And he was right. It's how I got so fucking good at what I do. Because of him, my dad, and that fucking shed."

Before I can stop myself, my mouth opens and the question comes out, "Who is your dad?"

E chuckles, looking back at me with a sinister smirk

decorating his face, "Welcome to The Exiled, Rain Sinclair. I am a Lord, my father is a Duke, and you, my little bat, are a Commoner."

I am a fucking what?

My brows rise, and my face has to be screaming *explain* because his response is quick. "The shed."

Pulling on my hand, E starts to walk and I follow, making our way to the shed, which must have been like a second home to him.

Unlike this monstrous home, which is very Montana in its exterior, the shed has white siding, gray shingles, with a white solid door and a silver handle. A similar keypad as the gate next to it.

Then I notice, it has no windows. For good reason.

Elijah places the pad of his finger on the keypad scanner, and then the lock clicks as it finishes scanning. His hand grabs a hold of the cold door handle and he takes a deep inhale, then blows it out slowly.

Pushing the door open, it's dark. Immediately, I smell dust and have a couple rapid sneezes exit me. No one's been in here for years, I suspect, as E flips the light switch on, a single overhead fluorescent light turns on, which illuminates the space. Nothing has been covered with sheets to protect the furniture and equipment. A thick lining of dust is covering the area.

We step in, the floor creaks beneath us, which is covered in larger white floor tiles, some of which are broken, and underneath you see the wood floorboards exposed.

A table takes up most of the space, and the walls are lined with the same cabinets and countertop that E has in Blackwood, along with a tiny sink.

As we step in farther, I close the door behind us. It's chilling how familiar the space is, but it must also be comforting to him.

"The Exiled is a society of very wealthy and powerful people who control the government and underground. From the police, to the mayor, and all criminal activities. If it happens in Bozeman, The Exiled knows about it and most likely is involved. Every five years, new initiates get brought in. We call it Hell Fire Night. We get free rein of the city for twelve hours, on the tenth day of the tenth month of the fifth year. During those twelve hours, we are free to do as we please, even more than we usually are.

"Locals have heard stories over the years, they usually prepare their homes and stay inside the entire time or leave. Tourists are naturally at risk, as they are blindly unaware. Sometimes Duchesses and Duke's, like my dad, give suggestions on what we do. Sometimes we get to decide on our own.

"During Hell Fire, there is a party in the woods at a giant home, done up and over the top. My personal version of hell. But the home is equipped with things we may need to fulfill certain plans. They are technically called sacrifices or party favors, depending on who you talk to. These individuals usually have been very naughty and must be put back in their places, then they are given an option: join us or die. If they join us, they are

Commoners, the bottom of the ranks; they do what we say, they are the bitches of The Exiled. I am a Lord, a born member. Hell Fire Night is to bring us into the ranks along with additional Commoners. At some point, the Duke's and Duchesses show up and watch as we play. But some members don't even make it to the party. They get carried away before showing up."

My eyes are wide as my brain tries to take everything in.

This shit actually exists. Groups like this.

Then again, my bio dad was the leader of a fucking cult.

"You are a Commoner, for now. We are fucking one. They will see that and you won't be called a Commoner for long. You are a fucking Sinclair. A Lady."

How is this my life? From a small town only months ago, to The Chapel, and now The Exiled.

Every moment of my life has been preparing me for this moment.

Each experience helps me navigate the next.

My mom would tell me to trust, and I am.

Logically, I should be freaking out. My anxiety should be in overdrive as my brain races trying to sort all these new details out. But my body isn't reacting that way.

Why?

He is my life. Where he goes, I go.

My soul and his soul. We are forever.

E lets go of my hand and walks over to the table,

placing his bat on it. The dust is disturbed and floats around him.

"This place, my shed," he stops and looks around, "this is where my demons became my friends."

With each pump from my heart, my chest becomes warm. His words touch me in a way I never anticipated. We all have happy places. Places that remind us of the good times.

This is his.

Then I get an idea of how to help him. How to keep this his happy place, instead of walking back into it feeling tortured and starved.

Walking over to the cabinets, one by one I open them up, looking for the perfect tool. So much of this stuff I had never seen before, but I want to know more. Another time. This is for him—about him. He needs this.

Opening the next cabinet door, there it is. Laying flat on the shelving, the steel is still shiny and the handle is matte black. Gripping it in my hand, it's cool to the touch. As I rub my thumb along the black grip, I know this is the right thing to do.

As I turn around to face E, the blade is facing him as the knife rests flat in my hand.

Two simple but powerful words leave my mouth.

"Cut me."

His brow furrows in confusion.

"If it's going to help. Do it. Please. Cut me. Make me bleed. Let me do this for you."

E shakes his head, "No. I'll be okay. It's only a few more hours."

His nostrils flare looking at the sharp blade, and his pupils dilate.

"Take it."

He swallows, his Adam's apple moves in his throat and his teeth play with his lip ring.

His hand reaches out, his thumb twitching as he hovers over my hand.

Moving my hand up to meet his, the knife is now between our palms. Looking up with E, I nod, encouraging him to just take it. You can see the internal struggle on his face, unsure of what to do.

Taking the lead, I reach up with my other hand and begin curling his fingers around the handle. He doesn't resist. Each finger is wrapping around it now as I let my other hand drop.

Stepping over to the table, I boost myself up as my legs hang over the edge.

Lifting one leg up I rest the heel of my shoe on the edge as I begin pulling my pant leg up. With my pale skin on display, I gently encourage him once more, "Do it."

His eyes take me in, starting from my head and moving slowly down my body.

"Why aren't you scared?" His question confuses me.

"Scared of what? You?" I shake my head. "I could never be. You would never hurt me on purpose."

"You know after tonight, we can't leave. Bozeman is

home. We can go back to Blackwood, visit your mom, but this is home now, little bat."

Tears prick my eyes. My mom.

Immediately I want to ask if we can relocate her here. So I can still have access to her whenever I need to talk to her. Or just be, sitting with her. What am I going to do without her? *Fuck*. No.

I can't do that to her. She's at rest in Blackwood, under a beautiful tree with flowers. Elijah did that for her —for me. He had no idea the impact he had by doing that, and he still doesn't fully understand how meaningful his gesture is by doing so. I can't disturb her over my selfish needs.

He has given up so much.

This is his time now. And I will just need to learn and adapt.

Rain, you can fucking do this.

Nodding my head, I say, "I understand. It's you and me, until the end."

The cool blade kisses my skin, lightly moving up toward my knee. Goosebumps follow behind.

"My demons will be able to come out and play more here. I will be free."

Tears well in my eyes, but I refuse to let them fall. I don't want him to realize the internal turmoil I am experiencing, it will only make his current situation worse.

He hates it when I'm sad. It triggers him.

I need this as much as him now.

"Press harder," my voice rasps, instructing E again.

His beautiful blue-with-brown-specks eyes are entirely focused now on the knife dancing along my skin. It looks like he is possibly spelling something out as he traces lines, but I can't make it out.

Then, without warning, he pushes. Only a tiny prick at first, where a bead of blood forms as he moves the blade up again. It slowly begins to drip down my leg. His eyes watch as it slides, and his nostrils flare as he takes a deep breath in. Before it reaches my shoe, E wipes the trail with his thumb and puts it in his mouth.

"So fucking good," he moans.

My sweet baby E needed this.

The cut isn't deep. He keeps it shallow the entire time, cutting maybe an inch more before he pulls back again.

As he takes the blade off my skin for the last time, he tosses it into the sink where it rattles before settling.

Leaning down, his fingers begin rubbing the blood along my shin, painting something abstract with it, I think. My eyes remain on his face, watching the expressions pass through him.

His touch and my blood are warm against me, his eyes are focused. He is happy.

Once satisfied, he steps back, admiring his work, then he nods for me to see.

Looking down, a smile forms on my lips. *MINE.*

"It's perfect," my breath whispers, as my hand reaches to my neck. My fingers faintly rub the vial, which encases the most precious gift I have ever received.

I am *his.*

I spend a few more moments admiring it before bringing my pant leg down, careful to not smudge it.

Looking back at him, his eyes seem brighter, happier.

Elijah is slowly coming back to me.

"We should go. We still have a lot to do before tonight. And I... We need to talk to my dad."

Jumping off the table, I grab his hand and lead him out.

Playfully, I joke, "You were the one that distracted me, mister." Winking at him as I finish the sentence.

He grabs his bat and follows behind. As we leave the shed, he turns the light off and closes the door behind us.

"Oh, little bat. You are in so much trouble later."

Sticking my tongue out, I giggle. "Good, I hope so!" His face is slightly amused by my antics while looking equally confused.

Before I can continue to bug him, he stops. My hand pulls on his, but he doesn't move. Instead, looking up toward the house. As I turn my head, I follow his eyes in the same direction.

Nate.

His dad is standing in a pair of dark slacks and a knitted sweater, looking down at us from the second-story balcony. Breaking the silence of our staring, his voice is firm and his words are minimal, "They are ready."

CHAPTER 5

ELIJAH

After my dad speaks, he heads back inside, leaving Rain and I still in the yard, alone again.

Her reaction to everything has confused me.

She wanted to help me.

I'll never understand why, but it felt so fucking good cutting her leg. Her beautiful crimson red blood beading at the opening of the shallow cut. As the wound filled with more blood, it became heavy enough to slide down, decorating her pale skin.

Fucking intoxicating.

It hypnotized me.

I needed to touch it. Play with it. Mark her with it.

But how I was able to stop, I don't understand.

Perhaps I do have some self-restraint when it comes to her, after all.

She didn't know I had control over myself, but she still let me cut her. Just to get a fucking taste of what I've been craving.

Rain Sinclair is a better person than I could ever be.

This withdrawal is a new feeling. Building for months.

At first it was sporadic, momentary urges which quickly subsided.

It continued to build each time I thought about it, pictured slicing a person's throat, having warm blood coating my skin, and my mouth would water.

The thoughts became more frequent. To the point where we were yesterday, as she sucked me off.

It would have been a beautiful sight, Rain on her knees, my cock in her mouth, with blood gushing out of her mouth. My little bat.

Now that I am home, back in Bozeman, with my dad and this crazy society shit. I will never have to go without for months again.

My demons will become my friends again and not my enemies.

Elijah Sinclair is home.

"I will have more questions about everything. But not tonight," her voice whispers as her breath evaporates into the cool mountain air.

I don't respond. It's not needed. Instead, I take the lead back and begin to walk us toward the house.

Entering through one of the back patio doors, we are immediately placed in my dad's office.

Taking a deep breath in, everything is still so familiar. The brown leather couch is still where I saw it last, but before it is a new glass coffee table. His large, dark wooden desk is the same, with built-in shelves behind it lining the wall. The carpet is new, along with the light fixtures decorating the space. But the smell is the same.

The office door is open. I can hear my dad's dress shoes echoing down the hall as he approaches.

My body is trying to react to this experience, my homecoming. It's fucking uncomfortable and I want it to stop.

Letting go of Rain's hand, my hands grip my hair, pulling it in order to focus me.

A low, intense growl leaves me.

What are these feelings? I fucking hate it.

My dad's hand is on my shoulder, I can sense his presence before he speaks. "I know. It's a lot at once and processing it is nearly impossible. Tonight. Just focus on that."

Nodding my head, I release my hair and open my eyes.

My nostrils still flare as I take deep breaths in and out. My mouth opens as I yell into the room. Pounding against my chest is my heart. The same heart that is making this all so fucking hard. Everything is coming down at me—at once.

My eyes shift around the space—I need her.

My little bat is now on the brown leather couch, her face looks like she's in pain. Her eyes are sad.

I don't like it.

Walking over to her, I kneel down. "What's wrong?" My eyes stare deep into hers.

Rain shakes her head. "Nothing. Everything is how it's meant to be. I'm okay."

I don't understand, but I accept it, for now.

Bringing my hand to her face, my thumb rubs against her soft bottom lip. Leaning forward, our lips meet and my hand moves to grip her face. It's a brief kiss but passionate. It sucks the air out of us both as our foreheads lean against each other's. As we part, our warm breaths meet again.

Her lips brush once more against mine before leaning back.

My cock hardens against my pants.

This fucking girl.

My dad clears his throat behind me, like it will have some sort of magical effect on me.

She is my focus.

He's been waiting ten years, what's a few more minutes?

Rain smirks, then pushes my shoulder.

Letting go of her face, I stand up and turn toward my dad. "Do you have the masks?" I ask as I adjust myself.

His eyes roll. "You seem in better spirits today."

My face remains unamused. At this point, the only thing I want to do is take my little bat home and fuck her until she forgets her fucking name.

"Your cousin, Francesca, has become a liability. We have placed a Commoner with her for the past couple weeks. He is acting like a boy with a crush, and she has fallen for it. Reports have been given nightly to his handler. Plans to expose us are in the works, primarily via social media. Our Commoner has a computer science background. He can easily handle that side for us."

Stepping toward my dad, my arms cross over my chest. "Understood."

Never liked the bitch anyway.

"Good."

Dad looks toward Rain. "You, my dear, will go into this evening as a Lord. You are a Sinclair. Never doubt that. You hold as much power as Elijah does when you step into a room. Own it. It's yours."

Tiny sniffles fill the room.

I don't care if he is my dad, if he has made her sad, I will punch him in the fucking face.

Rain's voice follows, "Thank you, sir—Nate, I mean. I'm sorry. But thank you."

My dad smiles, pleased with himself.

"Now, I trust my son has explained everything to you?" He questions, side-eyeing me in the process. Which is completely unnecessary.

"Of course I fucking did."

My little bat interrupts me, "E, be nice. But yes, he has told me. I understand what's expected from this evening."

Dad nods his head. "Excellent. Then all you need now are the masks."

Rubbing his hands together, he walks behind his desk and opens the side drawer. Reaching in, he pulls out two identical black rabbit masks. "The Commoner has plans to take her into the town center at nightfall. She is aware of what tonight is. She doesn't think we know anything, therefore she is an unaware walking target."

Rain rises and comes to stand next to me. My dad holds out our masks and we each grab one. The color of the masks also highlights the ranking: The Duke's and Duchesses wear gold, then the head of The Exiled—the Queen or King—wears white. And all of them have the identical emblemed engraved into the side, a rose dripping blood.

I'd prefer staying a Lord until I die, but eventually we will become a Duke and Duchess. But not a day in my life will I ever be a fucking King. Someone else can have that responsibility.

"And if the Commoner has to go?" I ask.

My dad doesn't miss a beat. "Then he goes."

I grin—then he fucking goes.

"It's still a few hours until nightfall. Go prepare. I'll see you both later," my dad dismisses us. As we walk toward the patio door, his voice fills the room once more, "Rain, you'll do great. You both will."

Rain smiles, looking back at him. "Thank you."

Saying nothing, I reach for her hand, holding it in my free one. Pulling her with me, I lead us out.

Rain yawns. "I could use a nap before we get ready."

Looking back at her, I say, "I'll wake you when it's time."

CHAPTER 6

ELIJAH

My face is buried between her legs. Her sweet scent is making my mouth water as my tongue laps her dripping pussy. Laying on my stomach, I've placed both her legs over my shoulders, resting on my back while my hands hold on to her thighs. Rain went for a nap after my dad's. To thank her for earlier, I'll make her cum all over my face. A soft moan leaves her mouth. Her body shifts as I stop moving, waiting to find out if she's woken up. The house is quiet, and her breathing is the only thing I hear as it remains heavy. Flicking her clit with my tongue, her hips buck slightly of their own accord. Bringing it between my lips, I suck hard on the most sensitive part of her body. Her pussy continues to drip down my chin as I lower one leg back to the mattress.

Patting my hand around, the cool object I am looking

for touches my skin. Gripping it in between my thumb and forefinger, I bring it closer to my face.

Rain's body trembles, her orgasm is nearing and a loud moan comes from above me. Hands grip my hair as she begins to use me, chasing her release, grinding her cunt against my face. Crying out into our room, she cums and I stop sucking her clit, lapping all her juices into my mouth.

Aftershocks move through her. Her pussy contracts with them, pushing out more of her white release.

Fucking delicious.

"Keep going. I need another one," her sleepy voice demands.

Pulling back, her hand is forced to release my hair.

"No, come back," she whines.

Her other leg is now resting on the other side of me.

My free hand grips her swollen clit and squeezes it as she groans.

Leaning back down, I kiss her lips, then take the sharp needle in my hand and push it rapidly through her clit.

Screams erupt as she rises, sitting up and looking down upon me.

"You motherfucker. What did you do?" she shouts, her face red and sweaty. I don't respond. Instead, I finish what I need to do. Pushing the sterile needle through her, I follow it with a gold curved barbell. And twist on the end once it is fully in.

As I look back up, she is pissed.

Her eyes tell me an assault of words is about to erupt from her mouth. Her lips part. "Don't you fucking look at me confused while your chin is glistening in my cum. You know what you fucking did."

She's right, I know exactly what I fucking did.

"You can't just do that to someone when they are sleeping. What the fuck is wrong with you?" Her shouting has turned into shrieks.

Sitting up on my knees, I grip her throat and push her back down to the mattress. My body moves on top of hers. A leg propped on either side of her torso as I look down. Her expression hasn't changed.

"Nothing is fucking wrong with me. You let me hurt you earlier. I was trying to show appreciation for it."

My breathing is heavy as I take in my little bat before me.

Letting go of her throat, my handprint remains.

As I jump off her and the bed, my eyes roam around the room. My thoughts are racing a mile a minute and I am finding it nearly impossible now to concentrate.

Why is she mad?

My vision goes fuzzy as my face feels warm.

A cool, hard object is now in my hand, then it's gone. A loud smash can be heard, as if it's miles away.

My vision is no longer fuzzy, it's black. My sight is completely gone.

Then a loud, deep yell distracts me. I'm no longer in control of my own body. A painful ache comes from my knuckles. As I try to pull my arm back, something scrapes along my wrist, down my hand and fingers. Once freed, I try to shake the ache off as another yell in the distance erupts.

A tiny hand touches my chest, bringing my attention back to right in front of me.

Followed by a tiny voice that sounds like an echo as she speaks, "Come back to me, E. It's going to be okay."

I feel too far gone.

"E, please come back. Listen to my voice. Follow it back to me."

Reaching out, I pull her warm body against mine. Her intoxicating smell invades my senses, vanilla mixed with coconut.

"Let me be your home. Your safe place, E. Please," her voice pleads.

The more I blink, the fog lifts and my vision comes back to me.

I've never been this fucking lost before.

"It's almost time. We just need to get ready. Then you can play. I promise." Rain's voice never shakes. She isn't afraid or sad. She is fucking strong.

Nodding my head against the top of hers, I don't need to speak. She knows.

My fingers rub the back of her neck, over the leather collar I gave her. That she wears with pride. Which has my blood proudly on display.

My eyes take in the space around me. A hole in the wall, and a glass lamp is destroyed and shattered on the ground.

Rain's hands grip either side of my face, forcing me to look down at her. Her expression is soft. No further words are spoken. I feel her inside of me. Reminding me I can control myself when it comes to her. The faith she has in me is unwavering.

Brushing my lips against hers, "My perfect little bat. Let's go play outside together," I say.

Her tongue licks my chin, tasting herself as a smile forms on her face.

"As you wish."

CHAPTER 7

RAIN

My heart was racing. Emotions were flowing freely, and my eyes watered.

Scared.

I've never been scared of him before. But today, I was.

E's face was red as his nostrils flared. Loud yells of terror echoed in our bedroom. Initially, I blamed myself. I made him mad. I shouldn't have reacted the way I did.

But then I realized, I was completely right in my actions and response. He was wrong, and he needs to learn how to handle that.

But instead, he reacted and I was fucking scared. He didn't blink once as he threw the lamp across the room. Or when his hand went through the drywall.

His knuckles are scraped, bound to be bruised surely. And a part of me was worried he would hurt me next.

I put my fear aside, for him. Sacrificed my sanity to save him. To bring him back to me.

It worked. My touch, my voice, and my presence. Slowly, he came back. As he took in the state of the space, he looked confused.

I wasn't scared anymore. Instead. Now.

I am just really pissed off.

This is almost as bad as when he casually changed my name to his when we first met.

At the same time, I am completely aware that this isn't fully his fault. He is unaware of how unacceptable this shit is. It's a part of his DNA and it will never change. So, I slowly inhale and exhale as I work myself through what just occurred.

The violence in our home is new. This goes to show how fucking on edge my sweet boy is.

After I brought him back, he even looked slightly mortified by his actions. The destruction, not the clit piercing. I then excused myself. We don't have much time left until Hell Fire begins.

I'm in the bathroom, getting ready. The sun has set and night has arrived.

"Elijah!" I shout toward the bedroom, hoping he can hear me from wherever he is in the house.

It takes a few moments, but his heavy footsteps make their way toward me.

Looking back in the mirror, I finish tying the bow in my hair, which I have left down, flowing over my shoulders. My ribbon is white and stands out perfectly.

I feel him.

Shifting my eyes, I see him behind me in the mirror, standing in the doorframe. His beautiful eyes take me in. I look down at his hand, his knuckles are still red. He needs to fucking ice them.

"I will after tonight." He reads my mind effortlessly, but I change the subject, not wanting to dwell.

"You said your dad was worse than mine. But so far, I don't get it."

Shaking his head, the corner of his lip lifts in amusement. "Your dad ran a cult. And wasn't shy about it. He made each move known. Loudly. My dad is calculated. You can never tell what's going on behind his eyes. That's what makes him more dangerous than yours. Flip of a coin, everything can change. With your dad. You saw his moves from miles away and I would just wait for him to play his card. My dad? You see his move just before he cuts your head off. And you wonder, how the fuck did I get here?" He pauses before continuing, "That is why my dad is more fucked. You like him, you trust him. You fucking shouldn't if you're not a Sinclair. Because one minute you're laughing with him, and the next your life is in shambles or you're bleeding out on the carpet. And you never saw it fucking coming."

Digesting his words, it makes sense. People knew what my father did and what he was capable of. But to be scared of the unknown is worse. A psychological game is far more terrifying. It makes you question yourself and your instincts. Paranoia would be your own demise and he didn't even have to lift a finger. I think I almost prefer that tactic.

"And now that I am back, it adds another layer, not only for my dad but The Exiled. I have an invisible collar around my neck and he holds my leash. The unpredictability of when he will let go of it places the fear of Satan in those around us."

"Where does that leave me?" The question is genuine. What is my role in all of this?

Chuckling, his tongue brushes against his perfectly white top teeth. "What people don't know yet? Where there is me, is also you. We have the element of surprise, for now. And tonight we will use this to our advantage with my cousin."

Another thought crosses my mind, sending me into a slight panic. "If we are officially part of this group, The Exiled, after tonight, does that mean we belong to them? You promised we could still go back to North Carolina to see my mom."

E walks up behind me, wrapping his arms around my bare waist, and looks into my eyes through the mirror. "We still make our own fucking rules. No one is ever going to keep you from your mom. My dad, knows not to restrict or limit me and now you. You are a fucking Sinclair, we do what we want, when we want. So stop worrying. We will always have Blackwood."

My fingertips dance along the light stone countertop, rolling my black eyeliner pencil back and forth. "Do my face?" I ask him shyly.

Spinning me around, his hands grip my waist as he lifts me up to sit on the counter. My legs wrap around him, pulling him closer. His hard cock grinds against my heat, which is even more sensitive now with the piercing. This fucking man.

"So fucking beautiful, little bat," his lips whisper against mine as we continue to tease each other.

Feeling cheeky, I taunt him more. "It's too bad your cock is on a pussy ban currently. Isn't it?"

His strong hand grips my neck. "The fuck you talking about? I own this pussy."

My lip curves, unaffected by his reactions. "Bad boys get punished. And you have been a very bad, bad boy."

His breathing is heavy and warm on my face as our eyes remain in contact. "And so do bad girls. I can play too, little bat."

My pussy continues to grind against him, taunting him further. His mouth moves next to my ear, whispering, "Keep doing that. If I can't cum, neither can you."

Then he's gone. The warmth from his breath disappears as he pulls back. Eyeliner in hand, he takes the cap off and rubs the tip between his fingers before beginning.

As he works, I watch his face. His eyes concentrated as his teeth play with his lip ring. E's free hand tilts my head as he continues his design.

These intimate moments are some of my favorites. Where it's just us. In complete silence, just being with one another, unapologetically ourselves. No matter where we are, we will always have these times. The one constant thing that will never change.

He turns my head slightly again as his eyes roam my face, squinting slightly as he analyzes his work. E adds the final touches before placing the eye pencil back down next to me.

Satisfied with his work, before stepping out of my hold, my legs remain wrapped around him the entire time, as I sit here naked while he turns my face into art. His lips connect with mine. A spark, a tingle, electrifies my body. Breathing him in, his familiar musky scent and knowing that I own him causes my pussy to drip. I need him desperately. His fingers go to my breast, rubbing them with his thumb before gripping my hard nipples and pinching them hard, causing my body to react against his. My hands rub against his covered chest, making their way up his neck then reaching his dark, thick locks of hair. I grip it and pull slightly. He growls into my mouth as a result.

Our tongues dance, battling for dominance.

Then I flip the script and pull back, my voice rasping as I speak. "Bad boys get punished."

His fist pounds next to me, mumbling under his breath, "Motherfucker." Which causes me to giggle.

"But I do have something for you, move and I'll get it." Pushing him back as I jump down, my bare feet hit the tile floors. E steps aside, letting me scurry into our bedroom, which still has the broken lamp in pieces on the floor. Stepping around it and hopping into the closet,

I push some of my clothes aside on the shelf and grab the tiny velvet box.

The fabric is soft against my fingers, and I smile with excitement as I rush back to him in the bathroom. He hasn't moved.

This is like Blackwood, the night we took my father down, but this time the roles are reversed. I wonder if he's realized? Thankfully the situation is vastly different, and we are joining his dad in something that appears to be incredibly important to E. Even if he hasn't said it, he also hasn't tried to fight it.

Nights like these signify important events in our lives, and it's good to celebrate and commemorate them. He collared me, and now I have something for him.

Holding my hands out, the box looking so large in my tiny palms, I wait for him to take it. He looks confused but intrigued as he takes the box.

Still holding it, he looks at me as I encourage him, "Open it."

Slowly, the lid opens and his eyes widen, with his head slightly shaking in disbelief. "When? How?"

I love giving gifts, and watching their reactions when they open them is the best thing.

"I had them made back home, in Blackwood. And brought them with me here, not knowing what was to come, but wanted them here just in case. Do you like them?"

Walking to the mirror, he places the box down and grabs the first fang out and places it over his natural fang tooth, but the ones I had made are longer and sharper. Checking it out once it's on, he takes the other and slides it on too. A giant smile forms on his face, showcasing his new accessories. My pussy throbs.

The fangs, with his face tattoo, are doing things to me. Fuck.

He winks at me through the mirror, knowing exactly what he is doing to me. "What a shame, we are both being punished. Otherwise, I would be teasing your sensitive inner thighs right now, letting my teeth tickle you as your cunt drips on my face."

My nostrils flare. I need his cock inside of me, stretching me to fit him.

Fuck.

E leaves the box on the counter and walks to me. His thumb and forefinger pinch my nipple, which causes my body to react.

"Finish getting ready. It's almost time," is all he says before leaving me alone.

Well played, fuck.

Turning, I catch a glimpse of myself in the mirror.

E has drawn exaggerated eyelashes under my bottom lid, along with my signature broken doll cracks. Smiling, I like it. It's perfect.

My outfit for this evening is hanging behind me. I put on the white crop top with thick shoulder straps and a square neckline. Next I slip on my high-waist white skirt, which is flowy and hangs barely mid-thigh. I contemplated underwear but realized my clit is too sensitive to have fabric against it. Lastly, I slide on my high-top sneakers, which are also white.

I take one last fit check in the mirror, satisfied with what I see, then go to grab my phone and head out.

Just as I pick it up, it vibrates in my hand. Looking down, an unknown number flashes across my screen. Hesitantly, I answer.

"Um, hello?"

A familiar, older, deep voice speaks from the other end. "Rogers heard a commotion earlier from the master suite, are you okay?"

I'm confused—Rogers is here?

"Uh, yeah. Everything is okay. I'm okay. He is just confused, on edge. It's so much change at once, he doesn't know how to feel. But it's okay. I got him, I promise."

The line goes silent. I look at the phone screen, thinking his dad has hung up on me, but it's still active.

"I know. In the past, it's always been only me who understood him. Who worried and helped. It's good he has you, Rain. I'm proud to have you in this family. He looks for you. I noticed that in my office earlier. He's changed, it's nice to see. But remember, I am here for you both. Anything. Please just call."

My chest warms with emotion. This man only just met me and has accepted me into his family, his home, and approves of me and his son. He understands E and never shames him. It makes me proud to be a Sinclair.

"Thank you." Is all I can muster up without

rambling as this overwhelming feeling of happiness spreads.

"Have fun tonight."

Then the call ends.

It's caught me off guard. Then I think back to what E said—is he being kind to throw me off? My eyes water at the thought. No, he's a good man. I am a Sinclair. He won't hurt me.

"Rain! Let's go. It's time." E's loud voice brings me back. Clearing my throat, I slide my phone into my skirt pocket and head toward the front door.

Let Hell Fire Night begin.

CHAPTER 8

RAIN

Walking to the front door, I find the lights are dimmed and E isn't here. Looking around, I can feel him but I can't see him. As I go to open the front door—perhaps he is on the other side—a hand wraps around my mouth, and an audible gasp from my mouth follows. With a racing heart, I squeeze my eyes, thinking, *Who is in my house?*

Fuck.

Rogers.

My leg moves backward, looking to donkey-kick whoever the fuck is behind me, but my foot is met with a solid frame because their legs are together.

I kick them again, hoping maybe I'll hurt them or take a knee out. After a couple tries, nothing. Then a sinister chuckle echoes in the space.

Instead of panicking, I start focusing.

His scent gives it away.

It's *him*. My baby E.

Just fuck, why am I so paranoid?

My heart pounds against my chest so hard and rapidly that I can hear it in my ears. Opening my mouth, I bite down on his hand, which is still covering me.

"Hmm, I like it rough, little bat," he teases, then licks my ear.

"I'm going to let go of your mouth. But I need you to bend over and touch your toes for me. Can you do that? Will you be a good girl for me?" His voice is rough and seductive and I am on the edge. My thighs push together and pussy drips as "Good girl" leaves his lips.

Slowly his hand inches away from my face, and I lick it before it's too far away, feeling possessive, marking what's mine.

"I'm not going to fuck you."

Blowing out a heavy sigh, I believe him. Bending at the waist, I can feel my skirt rising against my bare skin with each inch I move. His hand comes up, gripping and squeezing me as a faint growl can be heard. His thumb moves over the bite mark tattoo he gave me in Black-wood, and shivers crawl up my spine as he circles it.

My voice shakes as I question, "E, what are you doing?"

I can feel him smiling at the question.

"What if Rogers walks by?" I'd be absolutely mortified.

"He left a while ago. He was only here dropping something off for me earlier. Stop changing the subject and keep still." E's tone has become more harsh. He grips my ass cheeks now, it starts to hurt the harder he squeezes.

That's when I feel it, his spit, as it runs down the center. It is promptly followed by a cool, hard object entering inside of me. My body immediately reacts, clamping around the intrusion. It's the strangest feeling of being full.

E bends over me, whispering, "You will keep it in all night." I nod my head in response, as my brain is still processing what just happened.

The heat from his body is lost as he stands. I follow him slowly. The taller I stand, the more I feel it, the butt plug.

"Why did you think Rogers was here?"

Shit.

"Your dad called. To check in. He mentioned Rogers heard a commotion. I told him it was fine." I play it off coy, to not upset him or add to his stress.

I turn on my heel and take his face in. Reading him is a part of understanding him. E looks uneasy.

"Rogers needs to mind his own fucking business and to stay in his goddamn lane." As his final word is spoken, he grips his bat, which I completely missed leaning against the front entrance wall, and walks around me, opening the front door. "Come, little bat, we have a date."

* * *

The streets are empty. Businesses closed and the streetlights shine bright.

Reaching into the back seat, the plug moves with my body as my bottom rubs against the seat. Fuck, this feels good. As I go to grab the black rabbit masks, E stops me, "Not yet."

Turning back around, I sit, looking forward with pressure from the plug mounting. I need to stand up. But instead of getting out of the car, E pulls out his phone and starts to scroll.

What in the actual fuck?

Clearing my throat, I try to get his attention, but he ignores me.

Gazing out of the window, something catches my eye in the side mirror. Sitting forward, squinting my eyes, I see someone walking toward us. It's dark, making it harder to tell who it could be or what they are doing.

"Francesca just posted on her social media. Amateur. She's down the street, showing us she doesn't give a fuck what night it is. What a child."

Nodding my head, my eyes remained focused on the person, I murmur, "E, someone's coming our way." The words leave my lips slowly, filled with curiosity.

"Let's go." The car door opens, and E gets out before closing it behind him. The weight of the car shifts now that I am the only one inside. Even the tiniest movement causes the plug to move inside of me. Unable to stand this much longer, I follow suit and stand on the sidewalk. E is there, waiting for me, bat in hand. Faint clicks fill the silence surrounding us. As I look in the direction where it's coming from, I see an older lady with a walker casually making her way toward us.

Confused, I look at E who seems unfazed.

"Master Elijah, you have returned," a soft voice declares.

As she gets closer, I can make out her features more clearly. She is a shorter lady, with puffy white hair and a silk orange scarf around her head, tied under her chin. Pale skin, wearing a long brown skirt with brown loafers and a matching brown long-sleeve top. Her walker is the showstopper. Only meters away now, I see her walker is blinged out with purple gems, and it is officially the most wonderful thing I have ever seen. Frameless glasses sit low on her nose, with little to no makeup on other than bright pink lipstick.

As I take in this magnificent female, hoping that I am that cool when I get older, a thought occurs to me as I am wearing my white short skirt. "E, will people see what I have in?" I mumble under my breath, so she doesn't hear me.

"Don't care. But if I catch them looking, I will gut them alive then make them watch as I drape their intestines on you, like a necklace. You would look fucking beautiful. Crimson red running down your silk skin. Staining your white top. Fuck me." E pauses. His eyes hood as he bites his lip with his fangs while taking me in. "Then I would bend you over and fuck you raw." His voice is husky, and lust drips off each word.

Clenching my thighs together, my lips tingle and the need to grind against the plug is strong. Anything to tickle that spot, I'll do it. My clit piercing pinches, it only causes my body to react stronger.

Stepping closer to me, E wraps his strong, tattooed hand around my throat, above my collar, and threatens, "Don't you fucking dare try to cum. I'll latch a tiny gold leash from your new jewelry, force you onto all fours, and walk you around all night as my pet. Do you understand me?"

Smelling his musky scent, ecstasy ripples through me.

My tongue reaches out to his jawline and I slowly lick him. E's five-o'clock shadow is rough against me. But he tastes so fucking good, I wish it was his salty cum instead, but this will tide me over.

My breath dances on his skin as I whisper, "I understand."

His Adam's apple bobs as he swallows. I know if I were to reach my hand down to his cock, it would be rock hard. Before I get the opportunity to do so, someone clears their throat next to us. Breaking this moment of intense sexual tension.

Looking over, it's the older lady.

E steps back and looks at her nonchalantly. "Greta"

She smiles while rummaging through the bag sitting in the basket of her blinged-out walker. "Master Elijah. Welcome home."

Greta then looks at me. "Rain Sinclair, I have been waiting to meet you."

Her statement confuses me. I only just arrived, how does she know me? As I wait for her to continue to speak, a warm gust of wind dances around us. My hands hold my skirt down as I worry. Back home, this drastic change in weather could mean a tornado, but in Bozeman, I have no idea. My eyes look at E, seeing if he will react with concern. He doesn't. This must be okay.

"The weather adapts to them every ten years. Never fails. Hell Fire Night is not to be disturbed. It is a rite of passage."

Nodding my head, I don't respond. Instead, I'm waiting to hear what else she may share about this evening. I wonder if she is a part of The Exiled?

"I have something for you, Master Elijah. I've been waiting twenty years to give you this. Now come here, boy, and hold out that hand you just had around Rain."

Is this his grandmother, maybe?

E steps closer to Greta. Bending at the elbow, he holds his hand out and watches her carefully.

A silver object is being passed to him, and it looks familiar. I step closer, intrigued.

"Oh, my word. Is that...?" My breath hitches as I realize what she's given him.

A flat bar on one side, then ridges on the other make it so it fits over the fingers like a glove or a four-finger ring. Attached to the flat bar are five sharp claws. These claws would sit on the inside of the hand, resting slightly between each finger. They are meant to penetrate through skin and muscle as your hand wraps around your victim. It's called a bagh nakh, which loosely translates to 'tiger claw'. This seems to be an antique. And it is in perfect condition.

"It is Ms. Rain. I knew you had a passion for antique torture devices and that *this* would be perfect for tonight."

Elijah tilts his head. "The fuck you two going on about?"

Greta ignores him. "Enjoy catching your prey, she's waiting for you up the street with that bothersome Commoner. Perhaps he could disappear tonight as well."

With that, she winks at me and continues to walk past us.

Wanting to see the claw device closer, I go to reach for it, but E beats me and holds it behind his back. Fucker.

"Who was that?" I question, trying to distract him.

Shaking his head, he knows my next move before I even do. "Greta. She knows about The Exiled. She was invited to join, initiated as a Lady years and years ago, but she declined. Not wanting to be consumed by the life, but she loves watching and knowing about it. Greta sees it all. Never rats. So, they leave her alone. Greta has never been a risk like my cousin, Francesca. Her family was never a part of us, but she showed interest—potential, as my dad would say. Greta is one of the most fearless people I know. It's a night of terror and chaos and she is casually out for a stroll, giving me a claw. Legend."

Nodding my head, I take it all in as my mind races with more questions, to which I want the answers.

"We are in deep with everything to do with Bozeman, I told you that. Nothing happens that we don't know about. Counterfeits, gambling, drugs, police, judges, mysterious disappearances, infiltrating and planting people in places we need them. We can get in anywhere. And, if you are in this business and become a threat, you meet your maker. Me. And now you, little bat."

Fuck.

This is much more intense than my father's cult, The Chapel. Worry washes over me, the anxiety of the past day catching up as it all hits me.

"You will feel better once we get to the cabin. Where we will both finally get to play."

CHAPTER 9

ELIJAH

My bat in one hand, this claw thing in the other—fuck this bitch. It's going to feel incredible to gut her. Breathing in deep through my nose, I can already smell her cries. My tongue rubs against my fangs, now decorating my canines. Pushing it against one of the sharp tips, copper causing my taste buds to ignite with hunger. Licking my lips, our footsteps are drowned out by a whistle.

Looking at Rain, I find her looking at me curiously. Then I realize it's me.

What is going on? I don't whistle. I don't care enough to whistle.

"E, I think you're excited?" My little bat says while a large grin adorns her broken-looking, delicate face. My brows scrunch. "About what?"

Rain's arm wraps around mine as her fingertips trace

my forearm. "It's okay. You're mine now, remember? Let me help you." Her statement confuses me, but I leave it be as I hear a male voice faintly off in the distance say, "Come on, Franny. Not tonight. They will fucking slaughter you if they find out."

The Commoner. The prey.

"This is the one night they have free fucking rein on this place. No one would stop them from killing you here in the middle of the street. Fuck."

He's been compromised. This isn't a Commoner playing the part. This is a boy who has gotten his dick wet and wants to save her.

We stop, still out of sight of our prey. Rain turns her head back, eyes squinting. "She's gone."

Another gust of wind blows, and hair gets stuck on her face. Reaching up, I brush it off. "Nah, she's always around."

"You're being overdramatic. I am family. They won't touch me."

There she is. Overconfident. Because we will do more than touch her. We will make her scream, cry, and hurt.

"E, I have an idea. She doesn't know me. No one in town has seen me before. What if I go in first? Then you sneak around and come in from the other side. I'll keep them focused on me." My little bat is ready to play.

"No. You are not going in alone." My response is final. I cannot lose her.

Her nostrils flare as her eyes glare at me. Fucking stunning.

"Nothing will happen to me. Plus, I will throat punch the bitch if she tries anything. And I'm not talking about Francesca."

Looking up at the night sky, I blow out a deep breath, shaking my head exasperated. "Fine. Go."

Soft lips kiss the underside of my chin. By the time I look down, her feet are already carrying her forward. Absent-mindedly, my thumb rubs the cool metal of the claw as I continue to take her in. The pink gem at the end of the plug can faintly be seen through her white skirt as she walks under the lampposts.

As she turns the corner, I can hear her cheery voice mixed with the act of confusion when she greets them. "Hey, I'm new here. I live in the apartments down the road and noticed the streets suddenly went empty. But then I saw you two and thought I would come and ask, where is everyone?"

Swinging my bat in the air, it's finally fucking time.

RAIN

Both just stare at me.

Francesca is looking me up and down with looks of disgust and judgment radiating from her.

She is pretty if you like that full glam look all the time. Her entire face is done up, with smoky eyes, large fake lashes, bright blush, and contour, topped with a pale pink lip. Her hair is bright blonde—blood will look beautiful stained in it. Finally my eyes take in her outfit, an army green sweat suit paired with white sneakers.

It looks comfortable, I wonder where she got it from?

The man next to her must be the Commoner.

Sandy short blond hair, a chiseled jawline, with thin lips and bushy brows. He is also keeping it casual in black sweats, black sneakers, and a black tee. One arm is bare, and the other is full of ink. He seems like a pretty boy and is the first to speak. "You should go home. Lock your doors and don't come out until morning."

My head tilts, acting confused by his statement. Before I can question him further, Francesca speaks up, "What the fuck is painted on your face?"

Hm, well, she's rude.

With a smile, I politely respond, "The same shit painted on yours, makeup."

"You stupid bitch." Francesca spits out, then stomps toward me.

Her face is beautiful when filled with rage—passion. Biting my lip, impulse takes over. Reaching my hands out in front of me, they grip her face. She is slightly taller than me, but that doesn't matter.

She tries to pull back, but I dig my fingers into her cheeks as my thumbs hold her chin. I smash my lips against hers. This was never part of the plan. But plans change.

Our lips part as our tongues intertwine, dancing instead of battling for dominance. Kissing her is sensual.

My pussy tingles and I rub my thighs together, the plug and piercing add another level of torture inside of me. Tiny hands touch my skin, and fingers wrap around my wrists, but she doesn't stop me. Francesca's soft lips continue kissing mine. All the sensations are overwhelming, but I cannot get enough.

Before it can get any further, a deep and angry voice interrupts us. "Get your lips off her... NOW!"

All breathing has stopped, and our bodies are frozen.

Elijah.

CHAPTER 10

ELIJAH

My vision has tunneled.

"Elijah, man, calm down."

He's a Commoner and *he* thinks *he* has the right to tell me what to do?

Gripping his shoulder, I squeeze it hard. I can feel the sharp claw piercing through his shirt, then his thin lining of skin. Pressing even harder, the claws push through his thick shoulder muscle. Slowly, I move my hand while still firmly penetrating him from the back of his shoulder to the front. All while listening to the beautiful tears my claw is making. My ears hyperfocus on it. With each small movement, hearing the metal slicing through him. Fuck. My mouth waters.

As I reach the collarbone, the curved blades get caught. Warm, dark red blood coats my hand and trickles down my arm. The Commoner's shirt is completely doused in it.

Euphoric.

As the motherfucker tries to move, I pin him against the building's exterior brick wall with my bat under his chin. As his back slams against it, his mouth opens, releasing screams of terror.

Looking up, the bitch is crying. Drool is glistening down his face as it drips off his chin and onto my hand.

Seeing the look in my eyes, the Commoner panics, "No, no, no."

Yes. Yes. Yes.

Removing my hand from his collarbone, the blades are no longer silver. They are beautifully stained. I am going to devour him.

His arm hangs freely, along with the muscles, and I'm sure important ligaments have also been severed.

Smiling at the sight of my beautiful destruction, I shove my hand in his mouth, the warmth of his breath reminding me of the power I have. These past couple months, it felt like I had lost it, but it was never missing. It was waiting for me. For this moment. The buildup, the anticipation. Tonight, everything will be worth the wait.

My fingers hit the back of his throat, and his tonsils contract as he gags. "Throw up or bite me, I will make this last hours longer," my voice rasps with hopes he will give in to my cravings.

The Commoner's chest convulses, tears flowing freely. Sick of his antics, I apply pressure and destroy the inside of his mouth. Rotating my hand from side to side, I begin my assault on his tonsils which have been trying to keep me from moving. One swift movement in either direction, I slice clean through them.

My fingers follow behind, and blood continues to coat me as it flows down his throat.

The sharp edges then embed themselves into his tongue. Vibrations fluidly flow over my hand.

This is art. A symphony.

The vocal cords are telling me a story, singing me a song.

That they, too, would like him to die.

Reaching the tip of the tongue, what's left of it has begun to swell. But most of it is torn to shreds. And now, instead of drool, it's my favorite shade of red coating me.

Before removing my hand from his warm mouth, I flip my hand over and drag the blades across the roof of his mouth. The skin is incredibly thin. I can feel the tips grinding against the bone. This entire feeling is so fucking satisfying. Knowing how sensitive the area is brings me satisfaction. His nerves are on fire.

The smell of fear and the taste of their pain are the greatest hits of dopamine a man could ask for.

Gripping the Commoner's teeth, I make sure to get a couple of punctures into the gums. Another incredibly sensitive area. Each incision is like death by a thousand cuts.

Screams turn into muffled, incoherent cries.

Pathetic.

I don't respond.

As I take my hand out of his mouth, or what's left of it, you can't see an inch of my skin or the claw. I slap his cheek hard. The crack of his skin echoes in the bare streets. As I pull back, blood pours through the pierced areas of his skin that I just added.

Taking my work in, his eyes have become droopy as a snot bubble pops.

As I step back, removing my bat and forearm from under his chin, he falls, crumbling to the ground and curling into himself like an infant.

Having played long enough, I drop my wooden bat next to him, which is also covered in his sweet crimson. Bending at the waist, I get close enough so only he can hear me. "Roll the fuck over and bite it." The words come out, seething with rage.

The Commoner doesn't move. And I don't have time to wait.

Standing tall, I kick him hard in the ribs. Several cracks are heard immediately and I can only hope one punctured his lung, so he can choke on his blood while desperately gasping for air he can't get. At the same time that his ribs are cracking, he aggressively coughs up more blood, spitting it out in front of him.

Pussy.

"Now!"

Whimpers and cries begging me to stop are a moot point. When will he realize that I don't fucking care?

With unsteady hands, he attempts to push himself

up but fails. His shoulder muscle on the left side is completely destroyed, rendering him useless. Continuing to try would be futile.

Using his good side, the Commoner adjusts his body —head down, ass up—lips wrapped around the barrel. His arm begins to shake. The body is going into shock.

This motherfucker is going to be awake for this.

Positioning myself over him, one foot on either side of his torso, I lift my boot and push the sole of it against the crown of his head. Screams follow.

Stop playing, and just do it.

Her voice echoes in my head. My depraved goddess always gets what she asks for.

"Okay, little bat. As you wish."

Raising my foot, using all my power behind it, I stomp swiftly, forcing his jaw to crack and then break around my bat. Blood puddles around us as I go in once more. This time using my heel, I stomp once, twice, three times. I feel my boot get deeper and deeper into his head. Curb stomping the shit out of him. Skull fragments break off, and tiny pieces fall to the ground, soaking in the puddle.

He's gone.

Placing my foot back down, I don't move, my eyes still focused on the body before me.

My voice is deep as words come out slowly. "You are in so much fucking trouble."

CHAPTER 11

RAIN

He's back.

CHAPTER 12

ELIJAH

Still focusing on the sight before me, I contemplate my next move.

My body relaxes. The hit of dopamine settles.

Shifting my eyes slightly, her legs are shaking violently.

My gaze moves up. The shaking radiates over her entire body.

She should be fucking scared.

She should be on her fucking knees, pleading for mercy. Begging for leniency. Hoping *it* happens fast.

Taking a step forward, I slide my bat out from under the mutilated body below it. Bloodstains and indented teeth marks are visible. Swinging the bat with my wrist, I step forward. The sound of my boot hitting the concrete builds the tension. My face is neutral. Her back is against the building wall as her chin quivers. "You don't need to do this."

I don't *need* to do anything more than I *need* to do this.

The streetlight catches her face. Beads of sweat glisten.

Taking another step forward, tilting my head down, I rub my nose against her moist skin and inhale her deeply.

Fear is a beautiful scent.

As I reach the end of her forehead, I release my tongue and taste her.

Panic ignites on my taste buds.

Smiling, my fangs are sharp and pierce my bottom lip as they sit upon it. Licking my lips, I can faintly taste copper.

Not good enough.

I bite down on my lip harder. The skin is sensitive, and the pinch is satisfying. I can feel the warm blood trickle down my lip and onto my chin.

My excitement elevates again. Ready for more.

"You fucked with the wrong group of people, cousin." My tone is venomous.

Rain's hand comes between us. I grip her wrist with my free hand. The antique claw is still on, as it punctures her skin slightly. "Little bat, you have been a very bad, bad girl."

A tiny giggle erupts, with no effort to muffle it. My little bat is playing with fire.

"I like being bad for you, E."

Bringing her wrist up to my mouth, I rotate it to where I punctured her delicate skin. My tongue laps the area, devouring her sweet blood which drips down her arm.

Mine.

Thinking I am distracted, Francesca tries to inch herself away from us.

I've been doing this for fifteen years; I see everything.

Swiftly, letting go of Rain, I slap my hand next to my cousin's head. The metal claw scrapes against the cement, which sounds like nails against a chalkboard. She startles, stopping in place.

Rain takes this opportunity to step between us. Lifting her hand, she rubs her thumb against my cousin's lip slowly, taunting her. "Franny, it's bedtime."

Reaching back with her other hand, Rain grips my bat, taking it from my hand before stepping back next to me. A breeze washes over us, her hair tickles my arm, and my dick gets hard, straining against my pants as I remember she still has that plug safely secured inside of her.

My hand breaks free from the wall, and I take the claw off and pass it to Rain.

Then, in one quick movement, I flip Francesca around, holding her close against me as I wrap my arm around her neck while my other hand grips her head.

The arm which is wrapped around her grips the bicep of the arm holding her head.

The more I squeeze, the less blood and oxygen will

get to her brain, which will ultimately make her pass out. Much easier to transport an unconscious body than some annoying bitch screaming in the trunk.

Her phone drops as sharp nails scratch against me.

Using my strength, I lift her off the ground, her feet kicking into the air as her body continues to squirm. Taking my hint, Rain is quick to pick the phone up. This way, we can give it to my dad and his people can do whatever the fuck they need to do.

As Rain goes to stand, her ass adjusts as a small moan escapes.

Francesca's body goes limp.

I hold on a little longer to make sure she is out and not faking it.

We stand in silence.

Her body is heavy in my arms.

"E, I think she's out." Rain's voice breaks me from my trance.

Nodding, I maneuver her around in my arms until I am able to throw her over my shoulder.

Taking the lead, I walk down the sidewalk, leaving the Commoner's body behind. I don't hear my little bat behind me. What is she waiting for?

"E, shouldn't we hide him?"

Still walking, I shout back casually, "It's Hell Fire Night, just leave it. I'll text my dad to send a cleanup crew. No one is going to fucking care."

"Oh. Okay." Still hesitant, she begins to follow. Her tiny footsteps trail behind me as we reach the car.

Popping the trunk, I throw my cousin in, her body still limp, and close her in. Rain is already sitting in the car as I get in. Starting it, it roars to life.

Lifting the middle console open, I rummage around until I find what I am looking for, then toss it onto Rain's lap.

"Um, what is this for?"

Rolling my eyes, I reply, "Your lips."

Her voice is timid the next time she speaks. "Are you mad?"

Sitting up straight in my seat, I put the car into drive. My tone is deep and my words are sharp when I say, "Fucking furious."

CHAPTER 13

RAIN

"Only my lips touch you. You are mine, Rain! Never pull that shit again. Do you understand me?" His tone is chilling. It reminds me of the cave. I've only heard him use it while in the cave, as he was walking his mom into the fire.

That day symbolized the end of The Chapel, the beginning of our freedom, and his depression.

Did I push him too far earlier?

Kissing his cousin was based on pure instincts. I knew it would piss him off. It would bring him back, but did I push him to the opposite end? Was it too much?

To any other male or female, that shit had to look hot. I felt my body ignite the moment we touched. Being edged only made it that much more intense. But to my E, rage is what consumed him at the sight. As I knew it would.

And now, the Commoner is dead.

What I do know, for absolute certainty, is that my punishment will be severe and deserved.

Grabbing the sanitizer off my lap, I open it, squeeze some of the clear liquid on my fingers, then rub it against my lips. They shrivel, pulling tight and feeling dry immediately from the alcohol content in it. My instant reaction is to wet them with my tongue, which I regret immediately. The taste is horrendous. My face puckers like I just ate something sour.

"Good. Your lip shit is in the middle console."

It still astounds me each time he does something kind or considerate. This isn't a natural thought process for E, it takes a lot for him to think of these things and then to act on them. Watching his evolution into a caring psychopath has been one of my most favorite things.

Throwing the sanitizer back into the console, I find and apply my lip gloss. Hydration coats them and life comes back. It feels so fucking good.

We have already left downtown Bozeman. The car speeds down curved roads as we reach the outskirts. No one else is on the road but us. Our headlights dance along the thick tree line with each turn we make.

No music plays. We are driving in silence, with the exception of the engine roaring. Not a sound has come from the trunk. As each minute passes, I wonder if we killed her by accident.

"She's either passed out or fucking with us. She isn't dead," E whispers as he concentrates on the road.

Placing my hand over his hard thigh, I nod in understanding.

Our lights catch something briefly on the side of the road, almost like there are two eyes staring back at us.

"Deer. Fuckers jump out without warning."

My breathing becomes heavy as I focus harder on the tree line ahead, watching for other deer and hoping none cause us to die before our time. Just as I am scanning E's side, he slams on the brakes. The tires screech as we rapidly come to an abrupt stop. My body jolts forward as my seat belt locks, keeping me from flying through the windshield. At the same time, his arm reaches out in front of me as another safeguard. The wind is knocked out of me. My hands react, reaching out and hitting the dash. Tears prickle my eyes from the sheer terror.

A loud thump comes from the back, Francesca's body rolling into the truck walls. If she was still knocked out, she isn't anymore.

"Motherfucker. If I could gut him right now, I would." E is boiling, the words come out through clenched teeth.

Looking up, I see who—or should I say, *what*—he is referencing.

Dressed in all black, a person in a black warthog mask is standing before us, hands on the hood, as we are now idle, stopped in the middle of the dark road. Another moment passes before the person stands straight and takes off again through the woods.

My words come out shaky as my eyes continue to focus forward. "What was that?"

We both haven't moved from our positions.

"Hell Fire Night. The mask is like ours, black. I can't fucking touch him. He is one of us."

I can feel the urge radiating from him. The restraint he is showing is admirable.

Still curious, I continue, "How do you know who it was?"

"The animal on the mask identifies whose house or family they belong to. I know exactly who that fucker is."

With that, E's arm lowers, moving back to the steering wheel. I lower my own then readjust myself in the seat. My heart still races, as my body hasn't caught up to my brain yet.

"Your chest will hurt later. Most likely it will bruise. If he wasn't a Lord, I would skin him alive for hurting you. Then use it to wrap and bury Francesca in. You are mine. Only I can fucking mark you. Me!"

Reaching over, I grip E's strong thigh. "You own me. Only you. This was just an accident. I'll be okay, prom-ise." As I reassure him, I rub my collar where his blood rests safely in a vial.

One fang pokes out, biting his lip and re-piercing the small puncture he made earlier. A new coping mecha-nism. As the tiny droplets of blood bead out, it takes every bone in my body to not lean over and lick it off his lips.

Perhaps I will give him a little treat while we are

taking care of his cousin, to make up for his earlier aggravations.

Squeezing my thighs, my bottom joins as I grind slightly on the leather seat.

Fuck.

With my clit now decorated and a plug inside of me, the unfamiliarity of it all makes the sensations that much more intense. With each shift in my seat as I continue to watch his profile, the more I drip with need.

"I can smell you from here, little bat. You can't hide it from me, even in the dark." The corner of his lip curves as he presses on the gas.

We don't drive much farther before turning off the main road and onto a private driveway. A large, black iron gate looms before us as we pull up and slowly opens on its own. The windows of the car are heavily tinted, so how did they know to let us in?

"Sensor under the car."

The drive is made of cobblestone, lined with lights, shrubs, and thick trees. As we drive farther in, I look through the side mirror and see the gate closing behind us. E doesn't take it easy, he drives full speed down this incredibly long driveway. Where is the cabin? Looking out my window, my eyes try to take it all in but we're racing past so it's all a blur, impossible to catch a glimpse of what could be happening.

As I look forward again, a few parked cars begin to line the driveway. As we pass them, the cabin comes into view.

Fuck me. This is beautiful.

Elijah parks in front of the door. He doesn't give a shit and that's one of many things I love about him.

Love.

We don't say it. I doubt he even knows what it means or properly feels like. But he knows, and so do I. What we have is rare and one word will not define it.

My eyes blankly stare at the black front door as my mind continues to wander.

Something soft gets placed onto my lap. Looking down, it's the black rabbit mask his dad gave us earlier. My eyes wander to his, those beautiful blue eyes with brown specks staring back at me. I could get lost in them all day.

"Are you ready to play, little bat?"

CHAPTER 14

ELIJAH

With dry, bloodied hands, I reach into the back seat and reach for the masks. They are made of a hard black material. Not at all flimsy like the ones I had gotten in Blackwood. Taking in my little bat, I place one in her lap. "Are you ready to play, little bat?"

Her hazel eyes shine at the question before looking down at what I had just given her.

The lights catch the dark cracks lining her face, my beautiful broken doll. She balances out my crazy and at times, matches it. Rubbing my hand down my own marked face, I let out a deep sigh still taking her in. All fucking mine.

Rain's small hands lift it up as black ribbons hang from either side. Holding it to her face, she grips both thick pieces of fabric, bringing them around the back of her head and entwining them with her long dark hair, and ties it into a bow that matches the one already in her hair.

Mine is slightly different. Slipping it on, the leather strap, for which I pre-set the sizing, fits like a glove over my head.

Once both our masks are on, we look at each other once more. "I'm ready," she answers my unspoken question. Her tone is hushed, my little bat is nervous. She should be. Not even I have been to one of these fucking things before. I've only heard stories while eavesdropping on my father and his friends before leaving here.

Getting out of the car, Rain follows suit. I reach back in for my bat before closing the car door behind me. Walking around to the trunk, I lift my boot-clad foot up and kick it a couple of times while shouting, "Wake the fuck up, Francesca!"

Only silence greets me.

Kicking it once more, I give her a chance to stop playing stupid with me. I wait a moment. Still nothing.

Dumb bitch.

Looking at the taillights, I swing my bat and smash both of them in quick succession. Come on, bitch, take the bait.

Pieces of broken colored plastic break off my car and go flying to the cobblestone driveway. Francesca still stays quiet. If she is hoping I will give up and walk away, she has another thing coming. I was built for the long fucking game. I revel in the hunt.

Next, I take my bat, swing it over my head while holding it with both hands and begin to beat the top of my aluminum trunk. With each swing, loud bangs echo around us as dents begin to decorate my car. But I couldn't give a shit about the car. What's inside it is my prize.

"Francesca." *Smash.* "Wake up." *Smash.* "Nap time is fucking over!" *Smash.*

A high-pitched but muffled scream erupts from within.

Smirking, I can feel her fear rippling along my skin. I taste it on my tongue as my taste buds take it all in. My favorite meal outside of Rain is this.

Torture and murder after playing with my prey.

Reaching in my pocket, I press the button on my key fob and the trunk pops open. The light inside goes on as I look down at the pathetic blonde cunt curled in the fetal position, crying. Her face is blotchy and red, with tears covering her cheeks. Mascara streaks stain her skin.

Tilting my head, I simply watch her.

Little bat steps beside me. "I can't believe I kissed that."

Another loud whimper leaves my cousin's mouth.

"E, she's terribly annoying. Shall we go?" Rain plays the part perfectly. Smiling behind my mask, my fang nips my lip as I respond to her in my own head, *Yes, we shall, little bat.*

Handing the bat over to Rain, she takes it, gripping the handle tightly.

Reaching in, I grab the sobbing annoyance and throw her over my shoulder. Her body is limp as I do it. If she has given up this easily, that means my fun is ruined. There's no chance, she was ready to blow The Exiled up. Her fight will come back once I have her in my secured room.

Leaving the trunk open, because I truly do not give a shit—someone else can close it if they want—I lead us up the cobble steps to the large black front door. A large, bald man in a black suit is standing off to the side. In his hand is a scanner, and in his ear is an earpiece. Walking over, he places the scanning device overtop the barcode tattoo on the inside of my wrist, and it beeps once before he removes it. A green light goes off on the screen. He doesn't speak. Instead, he just nods at me as I go to open the door. He doesn't scan Rain, he must know she's with me. But we will still need to get her tattooed after. I've had mine since I started training with my mentor when I was five. It's part of being in this life.

Francesca continues sobbing as her lifeless body hangs over my shoulder. Stepping into what The Exiled calls a cabin secluded deep in the woods, and what I call a fucking mansion, shit music immediately penetrates my ears. As I take the rest of the space in, it's dark with large windows at the back. Wood surrounds us with a river running as the moon glistens off it. A large river rock fireplace decorates one wall, floor to ceiling, and is lit with a bright orange-and-red fire.

Oh, mighty dark one, we meet again.

Glad that fucker is dead. And his whore.

The farther we get in, the more insane it gets.

Black and red aerial silks hang from the ceiling. Looking up, one female and two males are doing acrobatics. One red silk is left untouched. Interesting.

My eyes continue to wander over to the second-story balcony. Duke's and Duchesses line the area in their gold masks. I see my dad immediately in his gold rabbit mask. My eyes continue to scan the room, noting the King isn't amongst them.

The King is the one we all ultimately answer to. I want to care about where he could be, why isn't he here? Or is he out lurking elsewhere? But I can't be bothered.

All I care about is that they are out of my way by the time I get up those stairs. As they stand between me and my playroom.

The stairs to the second story finally present themselves as I pass the large pyramid of metal wine goblets. Dark liquid fills them, spilling over the edges as more continues to pour down into them.

"E, look." Rain is next to me, pointing up. We have passed the aerials. Now when looking toward the ceiling, we find dead people who didn't survive Hell Fire, hanging upside down as their blood drains, dripping into the glassware.

Once I have taken it all in, I nod my head toward the

stairs. Rain takes the first step, as I follow. A flash of light hits us long enough for me to see the shining, jeweled plug still perfectly in place.

Reaching forward, I slip my fingers underneath her thin, short, white, and flowy skirt. Her hand is fast to swat me away, slapping my arm. I chuckle, pulling back and making her think she's won.

Not a fucking chance.

She still has a punishment awaiting her.

CHAPTER 15

RAIN

This is like nothing I have ever seen before. Not even on television or in movies. Dead bodies hang upside down from their feet, blood being drained from them. Loud music plays as people dance and snort drugs off the coffee table.

As we walk up the stairs, a female in a black shiny latex face mask with matching X pasties covering her nipples and a thin black G-string sneaks past me going downstairs. Her feet are bare as she scurries down. My eyes follow her, I'm curious and want to know more.

"Little bat," E scolds me, noticing I'm distracted.

The poor boy most likely thinks I want to snog her next. Laughing to myself, I have traumatized my possessive psychopath.

My gaze moves to him. His face is stone-cold serious, not at all impressed. Before returning my focus back in front, I wink and add a smirk, knowing I'll pay for it later, and I cannot wait. My pussy is throbbing, desperate to cum. I'm sure there is a wet spot on my skirt from it dripping the entire car ride here.

Reaching the top of the landing, I wait for E to take the lead. As he passes, I inhale his musky scent mixed with copper. My cunt is screaming to be stretched over his hard cock as the barbell piercing hits every spot perfectly. Picturing it, my cheeks flush. Thankfully the lights are dim, so no one else notices.

E turns left toward the balcony, which is still lined with a few of the Duke's and Duchesses, his dad being one of them because I can tell by the mask. Neither make eye contact with one another, their backs remain toward us as we pass behind. On the right side, I see a door with an all-too-familiar scanner. Putting his thumb up to it, the red laser analyzes the print before flashing green and the door pops open.

Bright light comes from the crack. E pushes the door farther, then walks in before disappearing inside.

I take in the area once more, the Duke's and Duchesses still have not paid us any attention. I am unsure whether that is normal or strange.

From the corner of my eye, the bright light begins to sliver off, the door closing. Not wanting to be left out, I scurry in.

The space is immaculate.

I notice two cameras in the corners, presumably for the

Duke's and Duchesses to watch. The room is painted black, with two tall black tool chests against one wall. Against another wall is a wooden shelf decorated with the most interesting tools. As my eyes move up, I notice many are antiques like I have read about, along with a few new-to-me tools. Then, all at once, my breath is taken from me as I let out a loud gasp, covering my mouth. I can't believe it. "A choke pear." The words are spoken faintly as they leave my lips.

A crashing noise is quick to take my attention. Turning my head rapidly toward it, I see E has thrown Francesca onto the hard surface of the table. Next to it is a matching black chair.

His mask is also gone, thrown on top of the tool chest. I guess we don't need to wear it while in here, so I untie my ribbon and place mine next to his.

As he ties her hands above her head, he casually says, "You said you wanted one," like this isn't a big deal. When it absolutely is—to me.

In the middle of this moment I am having with my E, Francesca decides to ruin it by opening her fucking mouth for the first time in over an hour.

"I have copies. I have sent them to others. If anything happens to me, they will expose you!"

E's strong, tattooed hand grips her chin, forcing her head to turn. "You are too stupid to have done that. And you love the attention, so for anyone else to have the glory other than yourself, that would never fucking happen. Remember, I am smarter than you. The fluorescent light in this room is smarter than you. It doesn't take much, does it?"

Then, it's like I am watching in slow motion as her lips pucker and then slightly open. A giant wad of spit comes flying out from between them and lands in E's eye. Another gasp leaves me, I am in absolute shock. She is truly as stupid as he just described her.

E doesn't move. Letting the thick saliva slowly run off his eyelashes as he opens his eyes. A large smile adorns his face, the fangs are proudly on display. I'm not sure I have ever seen him so happy.

Stepping back, his free hand reaches out for his bat.

I place it in his hand and he grips the handle before swinging it in circles by his waist. "You will wish it was the bat once I am done with you." His voice sends shivers down my spine. As he lets go of her and turns to face me, his eyes are pitch fucking black. They blend in perfectly with the black ink around his eyes.

I've read about this. I've wanted to educate myself as much as possible, when it comes to E and his condition and mental health.

Eyes turn black on psychopaths when they are excited or see something positive. It's like a trance, it doesn't last long and you have to be quick to catch it. Although, those with blue eyes are different. Their eyes turn black when enraged, which means Francesca is in for one hell of a ride. And to trigger this reaction from E, she deserves every bit.

It doesn't help that he has been contained for

months, only setting him on edge and pumping him full of emotions he doesn't know what to do with or how to release them. For someone like me, it would be a lot, never mind my E.

As he stands before me, looking into my eyes, I keep reminding myself, *He cannot hurt me, he won't hurt me.*

His bat drops on the tiled floor, bouncing at our feet before rolling off. The smile is gone and he isn't blinking. Through gritted teeth, his words come out harsh. "Tie her fucking feet."

As I slowly nod my head in response, he finally blinks. When his eyes show themselves again, they are the familiar bright blue with the brown specks that I love.

Raising his hand to his face, he wipes the spit off, and his smirk returns. Then *he* returns to me.

"Let's give the people a show."

CHAPTER 16

ELIJAH

I just want to sink my teeth into her tits.

My little bat is getting harder and harder to resist.

Grabbing the metal chain from the corner of the table, she closes the attached cuff around both of my cousin's ankles, ensuring her legs remain spread.

Stupid cunt.

Threatening me. As if I would believe the bullshit spewing from her lips. Did she forget what I just did to the Commoner assigned to her?

Looking down at my hands, they are still stained with his blood. I would permanently keep my hands this color if I could. Stain them daily by dipping them in a bucket with the harvested blood of those whose paths have crossed mine. To feel the warm, thick substance between my fingers. The same fingers that took them, to possess them.

Turning to the tool chest, I close my eyes. My cock hardens against my jeans as I picture curb stomping that pussy of a Commoner.

Fuck.

Months of suppression. And as a result, tonight I played a beautiful symphony made of blood and chaos.

The biggest weight lifted off my soul the moment I stuck the claws into his skin. Seeing Rain's lips on another person, regardless of gender, sent me there and gave me permission to stay.

Lately, feelings have tried to enter me. To confuse me and to make me frustrated, unsure of how to respond. The only person I ever allow in is her. I may never understand it, but she is my one and only.

My fingers touch the cool metal, gripping the handles as I open the drawers, my eyes are taking in the inventory and what The Exiled have provided.

My dad would have made sure it was properly stocked.

With each drawer I inspect, it confirms he did. From knives to clamps to nails, it all perfectly decorates the interior of the chest.

Swiping a large knife, I walk over to Francesca. The baggy sweater she is wearing has ridden up her stomach, exposing the elastic waistband of her thick matching sweatpants.

Gripping the band, I hold it tight and begin cutting

the fabric down the center seam. The knife is new or freshly sharpened, as it cuts through them effortlessly like butter. The thread pops off as I continue moving down, my hand gripping it to ensure the tension is maintained. Reaching her diseased cunt, I stop cutting just as the seam hits down her ass. Throwing the fabric open to each side and exposing her panties, a loud scream comes from next to me.

"No one here cares. And certainly no one outside that door. You know what tonight is. Screaming is point-less." Her theatrics are annoying me.

Satisfied with how I have prepared her, I take a couple steps toward Rain, who is still at the end of the table, waiting for instructions like my good little bat.

"The cheese grater."

Her eyes widen, pupils dilating, as she looks over my shoulder to the shelves. I know her mind is racing, I can feel it. But she knows better than to question me here.

Standing on her tiptoes, my beautiful, broken doll places her hands on my shoulders and kisses my cheek. The warm connection calms me. Relaxing me.

Then it's gone.

Wiggling her hips as she makes her way to the grater. The drumming of the bass can be faintly heard, but her gulp while reaching for it occupies the space louder.

Now she gets it.

"Now crawl back to me with it in your mouth, little bat."

I don't turn back to see her reaction. It doesn't

matter. What does matter, is that she fucking does what she's told by me.

Everything goes silent, even the annoying human lying before me. With my cock still straining against my pants, I hear her behind me. Shuffling around, trying to muffle her moans as the plug hits deeper with her new position.

Her palm slaps down against the tile with each movement. The distance isn't far, but Rain crawling any distance for me is a beautiful sight I am finding harder to resist by the minute.

Her head nudges against my leg once she reaches me.

Clever girl, I was curious what she would do with the grater.

"Such a good little bat, aren't you?" I coo. What I would do to shove my cock down her throat while watching her eyes water right now. Fuck.

Her eyes look up at me, eyelashes batting against her cheeks.

Mine.

Presenting my hand, her tiny one lifts up, grabbing ahold of it, using it to balance herself as she rises from the tiled floor with the circular grater still between her teeth.

As she rises, I notice something peeking through her top, a yellow lemon.

Having grabbed it without even being asked.

Rain's eyes look at me for approval, for more praise.

She is still being punished. Therefore, she will get what I give her without complaint.

"Little bat, take the cheese grater dildo and shove it up her diseased cunt." If she liked Francesca's one set of lips so much, let's see how much she likes the second set.

RAIN

Carefully placing my fingers around the grater, I take it out of my mouth and examine the shiny object. It is long —at least six inches, maybe longer. The end is hollow, it's almost as if they took a cone grater and molded it into a cock. As I rotate it, it goes from larger grates to small ones to the finest size. Even the tip is lined with sharp edges.

"She will scream. She will beg you to stop. You will want to, but you can't," E instructs me. He is right about all of it, except for one. "I won't want to stop. She wants to hurt our family. She's already dead to me." My tone is stone. I mean every word. I am a Sinclair, I am a Lady; this is my family too. Before stepping forward, E grips my hand and squeezes it, stopping me briefly.

"Francesca, I'll give you one shot. Not because I want to, but because my dad said I had to. Marry a Commoner, tonight. Join The Exiled, keep your mouth shut and push out ugly children—or die." E's tone is screaming boredom, which is usually how it is when he is doing something he has zero interest in, like offering someone mercy.

"I hate you. I hate this fucking family. I want nothing to do with any of you!"

Loosening his grip, that's all the permission I need to continue moving toward her covered pelvic area. E continues to taunt her, "I couldn't give a fuck either way. Although, my dad was saying how your dad, good old Uncle Greg, was getting sick of your shit too. So I doubt he will cry at your funeral."

Watching Francesca's face, I can see her plotting her response before E is even done speaking. Before she is able to spit it out, I gently move her panties to the side, exposing her lips. Lining the grater up to her hole, in one swift movement, with my hand firmly gripping the base, I shove it in with all the muscle and power I have.

My eyes stay open the entire time. As the air hits them, I can feel them drying out, but I don't care. I need to watch it all.

Francesca's back arches at the violent intrusion. High-pitched screams of pain and terror echo in the small room.

The girth of the metal grater isn't thin, it is easily two inches wide and penetrates her dry hole brutally without any lube. At first I am met with some resistance. Repositioning my hand so my palm is at the base, I push it in even harder. Gradually, it inches further inside of her.

Knowing how much E loves to watch, I don't want to rush it too much. I also fight the urge to twist it as it enters her, knowing this is just one part of a bigger game, which E had already mapped out in his head the moment we walked in here.

The rattling of chains follows each time she tries to move her legs, fighting the inevitable.

Drops of blood stain her white panties. Nothing dramatic, *yet*.

My palm hits her swollen lips, not from arousal but from pure torture. The cheese grater dildo is fully inserted inside of her. I leave her panties pushed to the side, keeping her exposed.

My eyes blink, restoring moisture to them and breaking me from my own trance. Looking up, Francesca's face is red and blotchy with tears streaming down her cheeks, leaving stains where her makeup once was. Racoon eyes have also formed. Bitch is a mess.

CHAPTER 17

ELIJAH

Pressing the quick release on the cuffs securing Francesca's wrists, "Rain, hold on to her," I say.

Caught off guard from taking in the sight of the aftermath of her performance, she scurries over to me and grips my cousin tightly.

She wants to question me, I can feel it. But she doesn't. Obeying the rules.

As I walk to my cousin's feet, I grab the lemon out of Rain's top, getting an idea, then kick the chair out from behind her, moving it so it's in front of the table. Squeezing the lemon tightly in my hand, it breaks and juice starts to drip down my fingers. Holding it over my cousin's cunt, I squeeze harder, coating her before tossing the remainder of the lemon over my shoulder to the ground.

Releasing each cuff around her ankles, Francesca

kicks, not realizing that moving her hips will only cause her more pain internally. By the time she does, more scratches leave her, followed by her legs falling back to the table.

Gripping both of them, I angle her hips up, holding her legs in the air, allowing the lemon juice to gradually slide inside and around her shredded, diseased pussy.

"No, no. It hurts so much. Make it stop. I'll do it. I'll do anything." Pathetic whimpers full of lies leave her. People will say and do anything to make the pain stop.

Not believing her, I don't stop, holding her legs up a little longer before I am satisfied.

Looking up at Rain, she smiles at me. "Little bat, keep a hold of her while I move her," I instruct. Her brows rise, eyes filled with excitement while nodding.

"We are going to put her in the chair like we did back in Blackwood, do you remember?"

A smirk follows. "Of course I remember."

Letting her legs fall, they crash against the table, causing it to bounce with the instability. Gripping Francesca under her arms, I lift her petite frame up effortlessly. Bending her at the waist, I pull her toward me off the table. A ball-aching, high-pitched yelp scratches in my eardrums.

With her arms bent at the elbows, Rain still has her wrists held tightly between both her hands as I swing Francesca over and onto the chair.

Loud sobs continue, guaranteeing that the grater is doing its job, destroying her from the inside out.

Keeping her legs spread, I strap both feet to the legs of the chair, then take over from Rain, securing her wrists behind her back.

Once satisfied, I walk over to the tool chest and open the drawers until I find what I am looking for. Hitting the top drawer last on the second chest, there they sit, shiny and new.

Grabbing both, I turn back to our traitor. "Hold her head still."

Rain grips both sides of my cousin's head. Stepping forward, I bend over. Reaching for her, I hold Francesca's eye open with my thumb and forefinger, applying pressure. Then I slide in the eye clamp, which is stainless steel and will keep her eye open. Once the first one is done, I move on to the next. It is a tad slippery from the endless well of tears, but it still fits in like a glove.

"Little bat, also in the top drawer are fishing hooks and white string. Get those and come back to me."

Once she has gotten what I've asked for, she stands next to me. "Now on your knees, sew her shut."

Taking in a deep breath, Rain pauses, then kneels down, moving her hips to adjust the intrusion in her anus, then crawls forward to Francesca.

"You can't do this to me!" Francesca continues to cry while shaking her body, again forgetting what moving will do to her, as it follows with absolute agony.

Sick of her bullshit, and being generally annoyed by her, I warn, "If you don't stop your bitching, she will sew those lips too. So shut the fuck up," I promise.

Watching Rain, she threads the hook with the white string and slants her head while examining the area and deciding where to start.

Her face is cute but serious. The only thing that would make this better is if my cock was in her mouth while she did it.

My eyes move to her fingers as the sharp hook is pushed into the sensitive skin, little bat picked correctly by starting from the bottom. As I watch Rain sew each stitch, I am captivated by her willingness and enthusiasm. The attention to detail is impeccable, each one is being spaced out millimeters apart for maximum impact and closure.

A piece of her long hair falls over her face. Reaching over, I finger it back behind her head then bunch the rest of her hair in my hand, holding it while I watch her finish.

There are two things in life I know: I hate when she's sad, and I could watch her do anything or nothing for the rest of my life and never get bored.

She is halfway up when drool drips onto her hand.

Fed up with my cousin, I wait for Rain to finish these lips before moving on to the next.

As her last stitch passes through the swollen flesh, she ties it off using a tailor's knot so it doesn't unthread while we continue to play. Rain leans forward, exposing her teeth, but I pull on her hair, forcing her back toward me. Letting go, I reach forward, taking hold of the thread and needle, and break it off with my fingers with a pull.

Bending down, my lips whisper against her ear, "Choke. Pear." My little bat's head turns toward me, eyes wide as she claps her hands together. I nod, encouraging her to get up and grab it.

Using my cousin's thighs to help her rise, the pressure causes her to squirm, which is followed by a loud hiss, knowing I am on my last fucking nerve with her. But the hiss doesn't get past my girl.

"You were gifted only with looks. Brains and logic were missed in your DNA string. You have been the most annoying person I've ever tortured and killed." Then my little bat raises her foot and places it on Francesca's pelvic bone, pushing down.

Mouth closed, her screams are still audible. Snot is continuing to slide out of her nose, and I'm sure tears would be flowing if her eyes weren't so dry from being forced to stay open.

Once satisfied, Rain removes her foot. The white thread is now stained red as the grater continues to cut her walls and cervix.

It only takes a few seconds before Rain returns with the choke pear, which she is absolutely captivated by, rubbing the antique torture tool while holding it close to her chest.

I had always pictured my little bat shoving this up our victim's ass or pussy, but the surprise of having the dildo cheese grater was too great to not use.

"Open your fucking mouth," I bark at Francesca.

Slowly, she obeys. Strings of saliva hang from her lips.

Rain wastes no time inserting her dream antique object once the opening is large enough. The choke pear is exactly how it sounds, metal-like spoon segments or that device doctors use when they stretch pussies for examinations. When they are closed together, they form the shape of a pear. Then coming from the top is a long key, which when twisted, spreads the spoons wide, expanding the pear wherever it is shoved, ultimately destroying and mutilating whoever has it inside of them.

The metal dings against Francesca's teeth as it becomes fully inserted, forcing her jaw to stay open and causing extreme agony.

"Any movement. Any noise. I'll turn the key," Rain threatens. Francesca doesn't respond or acknowledge her, her chest simply heaves in terror. This pleases my little bat. "Good job listening. Because you are really starting to annoy me. And I am the nice one. It would help you to remember that."

She then turns to me, and her hands grip mine. "It fits perfectly. Just how I imagined it. Thank you, E." Her lips then brush against mine. The tip of her tongue flicks my top lip, teasing as we continue to edge each other.

As she steps back, she turns around to admire her work. In one swift movement, I slap her ass. My hand connecting to her causes her to jump and then moan. Rain then moves her hands to her backside, covering herself in an effort to stop another slap.

Oh, little bat. More is coming. Just not how you expect it.

Bending over, my bat is lying next to me, which I grab ahold of. Then eyeing each camera, I decide that the show is over. Walking to each corner, I swing the wooden bat and take out the cameras watching us. The cameras smash, and tiny pieces of plastic go flying.

This show just turned private.

CHAPTER 18

RAIN

Adrenaline courses through my veins. It's warm and electric. My fingers are tingling with anticipation. Biting my lip, my mouth waters as I watch him.

This isn't like the others.

E is in his element here. Finally back home.

"Back on your knees, little bat. And take my cock out," E instructs while walking over. I have never found him as attractive as I do right now.

Absolute power and dominance.

As I lower myself back to the ground before E, he points his bat at his cousin. "If you stop looking or move your head, I will take out your eyes with a melon scooper, then shove them up your own asshole. But it wouldn't stop there. While you are still bent over, I would hot-brand your ass shut. And you wonder why I would do this? Because I fucking can." He slams his bat down on the table behind her. The loud bang causes her body to jolt.

My pussy drips. Spit flies out of his mouth onto her face with each clear, distinct word. They are spoken with intention, not threats.

That's my man. My psychopath.

My knees hit the cold, tiled floor. Looking up at him, his strong jawline and face are decorated with beautiful black ink. I just want to reach up under his shirt and rub his soft skin while sucking on his cock.

His head turns, catching me admiring him. His demeanor changes, and his face becomes softer.

"Lift your skirt up, little bat. Show me my pussy."

I need him inside of me.

Taking the thin white fabric between my fingers, I lift my skirt up, tucking the hem into my high waistband and putting myself on display.

Stepping in front of me, he turns to the tool chest, rummaging through the drawers until he finds what he needs. I can tell when he has found it. The bat drops, bouncing off the floor before rolling next to me. The contact causes my skin to chill. Goosebumps rise as my lips continue to throb between my legs.

E's fist is clenched, while his other hand touches my chin, raising my face to look up at him. Opening his closed hand, a thin gold chain falls. "Clip it to your clit."

My eyes stay on his as my hand finds the cool metal. Pinching the clasp open between my fingers, my hand moves to my heat. Two of my fingers spread me open, exposing my new piece of shiny jewelry attached to my swollen clit. It's been painful but also so fucking good.

What they say is true, beauty is pain and pain is pleasure.

Sliding the edge of the clasp opening under my gold ring, it hooks on effortlessly as I release my hold. E still holds the other end.

"Collared and leashed. My beautiful little bat," his voice rasps, lust falling from his lips as he admires his pet.

Our guest gags.

My face goes from soft to furious, turning my neck, I'm shocked I don't give myself whiplash from it. "Shut the fuck up! Elijah has been generous with you. I have been more than fucking fair. You decided not to join the family. There are consequences to your actions. Not even your daddy wants to save you. You are going to die. How painfully it ends is up to you. Now, do you fucking mind, my man is trying to be romantic!"

How fucking dare she judge? Be rude? My blood is boiling, I can feel my face radiating heat. My cheeks are flushed.

His large hand grips my face, bringing my focus back to him.

"You kissed what's mine. I had to watch that. Now you get to watch this." As the last word leaves him, he begins to undo his zipper. My body has been craving this since we left the house. My bottom wiggles, moving the plug still inside of me around.

"Don't move. I know what you're doing. Take me out."

My fingers rush for his button, undoing it then pulling his pants down to his knees. E isn't wearing underwear. His large, pierced cock springs out, hard. His head is dripping with delicious precum. His dark shirt hangs low, but I desperately need to see more of his inked skin. To touch and feel it against my fingertips.

The light bounces off his silver piercing, captivating me.

"Little bat, on all fours." My eyes look back at his. I nod once, acknowledging him. Keeping my focus on him, leaning forward, I place both palms to the ground while perking my ass up behind me, which is exposed.

With raised brows and a stone face, he gives me what my body craves. "One lick only."

Bastard is still edging me.

As I stick my tongue out, I reach his swollen head but he steps back. A whimper leaves me. Fucker.

Moving on my hands and knees, I inch forward and try again.

Please let me have you.

He knows I am desperate, my face surely isn't hiding anything, but that doesn't stop him from taking one more step. I follow again. This time as my tongue goes to graze him, he stays in place. My taste buds ignite at the contact. The saltiness of his precum is everything I've been yearning for.

My peripheral catches his hand moving. Softly he

rests it on top of my head, petting and praising me, "Such a good little bat. Do you like when I make you crawl? Tease you with my cock?"

I go in for one more lick, but he scolds me, "Tsk, tsk, little bat. I said just one lick."

My mouth waters, but I swallow in defeat.

E's knees bend, and his cock hits the side of my face. The contact sends my body into an internal frenzy, begging to be released.

He clasps the end of the leash to my collar, which contains his blood. E's lips brush against my cheek as he whispers softly against my skin, "I'll be coming first."

My face drops, this is going to be excruciating. Even my breasts are throbbing. My nipples are hard and starting to ache.

As painful as this is, it was worth kissing her to see him destroy that boy on the streets. To have his hands stained in beautiful crimson. To be played with and worshiped while being punished perfectly.

CHAPTER 19

ELIJAH

She isn't getting away with it.

Walking behind her, I kneel down and push her face down against the tile, thrusting her ass in the air. Her butt plug is still lodged in place between her perky cheeks. The pink gem glistens as the fluorescents bounce off of it.

"You will never place your lips on another fucking person. You. Are. Mine." As the last word spits out of my mouth, my free hand grips my hard cock, lining the tip up to her entrance. Thrusting my hips, I slide inside of her, raw.

A muffled moan immediately follows as I continue to force myself inside of her. Using her shoulder as support, I pull her body back as I pound forward. Her slick slit allows me to slide in with minimal resistance. The feeling of her pussy stretching around my cock turns me into a savage.

Rain continues to whimper. She's been horny for this since we left the house. "Ah. Fuck."

She is tight as her walls clamp around me. I watch as I move in and out of her, my pelvis slapping against her ass. Her cheeks jiggle with each hard thrust inside of her.

"Do we need to take you to church, little bat? Cleanse you of your sins?"

Panting, she says, "No, I'll be your good girl, E. Promise. I won't do it again. My lips are yours. Only yours," she promises.

Gripping her hair, I wrap it around my fist and pull it hard. Her neck arches back as her head lifts off the ground, and a loud yelp follows. "I own every part of you. Do you fucking understand?"

She pants, breathless as she continues to fight her building orgasm, "Yes. I'm sorry. All of me, E. It's yours. I am yours."

I release some of the tension, but I keep ahold of her hair as I continue to fuck her mercilessly. My cock begins to swell, and I can feel her cunt clamp around me tighter. "You're not allowed to cum, little bat. Don't even try," I command as I slap her ass, hard. I can feel my hand tingle as our skin connects. Another yelp leaves her between moans of torture, desperate like a whore desperate to cum. Removing my hand, her pale skin reddens, as my print is left behind. Seeing it provokes me, and my chest fills with pride, because I fucking own her. Only I can do this to her. If anyone else tries to get close, I'll gut them and leave them to die and rot in a hole six feet under.

My balls tighten as the familiar tingle moves down my back and through my legs. Working her harder, my cum shoots out, coating her walls. Her pussy keeps trying to milk me, but she tries to stop it each time it begins.

As I pull my cock out of her, I instantly miss being inside of her, but I have other plans.

Eyeing her plug, I pull it out, tossing it to the floor. As the metal toy bounces from the impact, it pings against the title, then rolls next to my bat. With my cock gripped in my hand, I can feel both of our juices coating me. I jerk myself off as I continue to cum on her ass, glazing her perfectly. Some drips inside her stretched hole as I use my other hand to rub my release all over her skin. My little bat will feel me all over her until I tell her she can clean it off.

Sticking my thumb inside of her hole, her hips buck as I finger her.

"E, please, please let me cum. I'll be good. I promise," she begs, panting. Her body is shaking from withdrawal. I've been edging her for hours, one more flick of her clit and she will be done for.

The last bit of my orgasm decorates her as my thumb plays with her rim. Cries of need escape from between her lips. I take in the beautiful sight before me, her hair a mess, face down ass up, wearing white. Ignoring her moans, my eyes land on the red tattoo of my teeth which I did only months ago to her.

I let my cock go and grip her butt cheek, holding it tightly in my hand. My dick hangs between my legs as I bend over. Opening my mouth, my fangs graze her skin and goosebumps appear. I position my mouth below the tattoo and just as I bite into her, I speak one word, "Cum."

Rain's skin pops as my teeth break the surface. Loud moans echo. Her puckered hole grips me as her back arches. My tongue licks the dripping blood which is also mixed with my salty release, and it lightly coats the inside of my mouth as I bite harder.

Through heavy breaths, she moans, "Fuck, E, squeeze my breasts. Please. They are aching."

Bringing my mouth up, I admire my work. Her skin is bright red around the new marks, which drip that perfect shade of red I crave. Taking my thumb out of her, I slowly move it down her slit. She is soaked, dripping as I slap her swollen lips. Her hips buck as she hisses.

Bringing my hand back out, I flip her tiny frame over in one rapid movement, placing her on her back. The gold chain is draped over her chest. Her face is flushed with hooded eyes as her legs have fallen to either side, putting her wet pussy on display for me.

It takes all my self-restraint not to bend down and cover my face in her. My tongue is itching to lick between her folds, to taste her sweet release against my taste buds. But she is still being punished, because my little bat was a bad, bad girl.

Moving my hands, they cup each of her breasts

which are heavy and more swollen than usual. Her arousal is seen and her nipples get harder as my thumbs circle them. Taking them between my thumbs and fore-fingers, I pinch them, hard. Rain's face turns to the side as another loud moan leaves her. "Fuck. More. Just like that, E."

I stop immediately. My hand moves and grips her chin, forcing her to focus back on me. "No. This isn't for you. Not this time," I remind her. She swallows while nodding in understanding.

"Good girl."

Leaning forward, my nose brushes against hers. Warm breath tickles me as my lips touch hers. Her mouth opens for me as our tongues dance, mine demanding and taking dominance. I can feel my cock getting hard again as my pelvis rocks against her center. Rain wraps her legs around my hips and I let her believe I get lost in the moment, but I don't.

Nipping at her lip, I tug it and then let go. Her tongue sneaks out, licking the same place, then biting it. "We have a job to finish, little bat. We are not finishing this." I pause to look down at her body. "If you are good, we will finish this later."

Her face falls, disappointed that I won't give in. But it doesn't bother me.

Sitting up on my knees, I shove my hard, throbbing cock back into my pants and zip them up. I help and untuck her skirt from her waist to cover her up. I don't let her clean up.

As I rise, I place my hand out. She grabs ahold of it and follows. Standing next to me, Rain catches me off guard. Tiny fingers hold my face as my little bat rises to her tiptoes, sticking her tongue out. She licks my cheek from chin to eye with the tip of her tongue and looks at me. "Mine."

CHAPTER 20

RAIN

My pussy still aches. I desperately miss the feeling of him inside of me already. I need to cum around his cock. Once was not enough.

Doing this, licking E, is my way of showing him who he belongs to. His smirk after saying *Mine* shows me he likes it.

As my skirt settles back down, my chain pulls on my clit. E notices it is also causing the front of my skirt to rise. Reaching forward, he unclips it from my collar and wraps the delicate chain around his wrist. The gesture is romantic, whether he realizes it or not.

Our souls were lost without each other. Now that they have been found, we are never letting go. He will forever own me. I am his pet, he is my owner, and I will worship him and us until my last dying breath.

With my hand on his chest, I burrow myself into his side.

His musky scent, mixed with sweat, is comforting.

E's focus moves back to his cousin. Her face is pale and I wonder if she's still alive. Watching her chest, it moves slowly up and down. My eyes move down her body to her sewn lips, the thread is absolutely drenched now in blood, which gives me an idea. But I wait; this is E's domain, so I let him take the lead.

"I can see your eyes looking. Wandering." His rough voice breaks the silence. My focus moves back to him. Curious, I wait for E to continue.

"I have one too." He lifts his long sleeve, exposing his inked arm and bat tattoo at the forefront.

"It means that the devil is on our side. And that you should be very fucking concerned about that."

If I didn't know him, I would be terrified. His tone has completely changed from how it was with me, to her.

Francesca's reaction is hard to tell, I'm not sure if her lip is faintly trembling because of the choke pear or because she is now getting it, she is now fucking terrified.

E tilts his head down, looking at me with soft eyes. "Little bat, I can feel you thinking."

Smiling, he always knows.

"The thread is coated in blood. Sitting on it at that angle must be tearing her insides apart. If she wants the grater out, she should have to take it out herself, don't you think? It will ruin her coming out, but then, it's out." I'm not confident in my idea, or that he will like it. His face doesn't tell me anything as I wait for a response.

Keeping his focus on me, he speaks, "For every thirty seconds she doesn't have it out of her, you turn the choke pear key. She either leaves here with a broken jaw or with a torn-up, diseased pussy. Let her pick. What do you think of that, little bat?"

Eagerly I nod, loving this idea. I'm giddy with excitement—finally, I can use my choke pear!

E steps toward her, our contact breaking and his warmth gone.

For a moment, I forget he is holding the chain, my leash. As he goes behind the chair, it pulls, and my clit piercing is yanked. Pulling at my sensitive numb, causing me to hiss, and my eyes water from the sting of it. I move my feet and rush to be next to him to stop the pain. E isn't fazed, still undoing the restraints around her wrists. As the clasp comes undone on them, he tsks. "Could have avoided all of this, if you would have just shut up. But you couldn't and now some Commoner fucker is going to have to clean your jaw off the floor."

Placing my hand on his shoulder, I add, "Or her bloody cunt," not wanting her to lose complete hope yet. But I do wish it is her jaw that wins.

"Oh, and the clamps are staying in your eyes," he adds as her wrists become freed.

Francesca doesn't move, perhaps she thinks this is a trick or she is genuinely terrified. E doesn't wait even a second before encouraging her to begin. We walk to his bat which lays on the ground, picking it up, and I see where he's looking. In the next breath, it is being swung and connects with one of the back legs of the chair, knocking it out from under her. Not expecting it, she topples over with her legs still connected. A loud, muffled scream tries to leave her mouth. The side of her face hits the floor, and the clamp in her eye lodges inside the socket, piercing her eyeball. The choke pear remains in place, but more blood comes from her cunt. The grater dildo definitely does more damage internally.

"Ten seconds left," E taunts.

Francesca's one arm is trapped underneath her. Using all the energy she can muster up, she shimmies her arm toward her waist as her other hand begins working frantically. Her fingers try to undo the knot which is now blood-soaked. Pulling on the thread only makes it worse, tightening it further.

E taps my hand—it's time.

Stepping next to her face, more moans of agony spew out of her. Taking a bent knee, I take the cool metal key into my hands and give it one big twist, completing a full circle. You can hear the springs crank as I go. The spoons click up one notch, which begins the process of fully opening.

Patting my head, E signals me to stop. We must wait another thirty seconds. As we do, her eye starts to bleed with the pressure mounting on the clamp being pushed in.

Francesca is able to get her other hand free enough to

help, but it's of no use. She isn't getting the thread out unless we cut it. Her fingers slip along it, at one point even making a squeaking sound as they rub.

Looking up at E, he nods.

My fingers twist the key once more, opening it further. It's like a balloon in her mouth, each turn is akin to blowing air into it. Eventually, the metal spoons will be at capacity, and her jaw will snap from the pressure of not being able to open any further and pop, just like a balloon.

This cycle continues a couple more times.

Her fingernails scrape against the thread now, trying to thin it out.

With each turn of the key, Francesca's cries of pain become more audible, the choke pear forcing her mouth open only helps project her screams.

Looking up, her eye is completely red, presumably her vision is gone from that side.

Tapping his boot-clad foot, E casually mentions, "I'm getting bored."

Francesca is fucked. A bored E, is a bad fucking E.

Reaching in his pocket, he pulls out his switchblade and flicks it open. Joining me on the floor, he tilts his head at the sight before him. "Fucking pathetic. You did nothing in the time we gave you. You fucking deserve this. Useless bitch."

The sharp blade connects with the soaked thread. As E starts at the bottom, he works his way up, slicing each stitch open one by one. The thread gets caught a couple times on the blade, pulling on her lips and causing additional pain.

He gets to the last one and I decide I will not be left out.

At the same time as the final stitch comes undone, I twist the key on the choke pear. Needing to put all my strength behind this turn as the pressure and resistance try to fight back. And the best part is, E doesn't stop me.

I yell with my momentum. My body moves with the motion of my hands, turning the key counterclockwise. The soles of my shoes squeak against the floor. I hear the snap of thread, and then the choke pear follows. This time instead of it clicking as it moves up, it's her jaw cracking. My ears ache as her scream is piercing my eardrums.

The vibrations of her jaw bones and muscles being stretched to the max can be felt as I keep my fingers on the key. Her jaw tries to fight back, but I keep the pressure. Seconds later, a loud pop follows.

I fucking love this. Imagine the damage if I shoved it into one of her other holes.

I am addicted. Biting my lip, the feeling brings satisfaction over me, along with excitement. I need to do this again.

But that's not all. We aren't done with the traitor bitch.

I fall backward as I let go of the key and as I glance at E, I can feel he isn't finished.

Tossing the blade beside him, he grips the cool metal

rim of the grater and deliberately begins to turn it, unhurried, while it is still lodged deep inside of her.

My hands cover my ears, blocking out her cries, not because I don't like it, only because her vocal cords are destroying my ears. My ears feel more sensitive than usual, perhaps it's the small room we are in and the sound bouncing off the four walls which enclose the space.

Francesca tries to fling her body around, an effort which is proven to be pointless as she is still attached to the chair.

I could watch E work all day and never get bored. My man at work is a sight, I clench my thighs together. My pussy is dripping as I watch his face, it's stone cold. His eyes never blink. His breathing is leveled. E is in his element. He was born for this moment. And all the others like this.

The grater is hollow, his fingers slip inside of it, and his arms flex as he applies pressure. The screams no longer bother me, they sound like they are miles away as I concentrate on him. Watching him work. Then, inch by inch, the grater begins to come out of her. Blood drips down his hand, trails of it branch off down his forearm and begin dripping to the ground.

Torn skin and muscle are attached to the sharp ridges as more of the dildo becomes exposed. A stray piece of thread that hangs from her lips, still attached, gets caught. E doesn't care, he keeps it attached as he continues to drag the grater out. It pulls and another whimper of distress penetrates our ears.

E twists it once more before dislodging it from her opening. You can hear it scraping her insides. The tip has smaller, more prickly and sharper bits. This final move is absolutely tearing her apart.

"We will need our masks back on after this is out." His voice is calm, not commanding. Regardless, I stand to grab them for us off the tool chest, preparing for whatever he has planned. Looking back at Francesca, long strings of drool mixed blood hang from her mouth and the metal of the choke pear.

Bitch is ruining my new toy.

"I'll get you another one," he says casually as the tip of the grater starts to become visible.

Our connection only grows stronger. He always knows what I'm thinking, the same way as I can feel him.

As the tip comes out of her, the metal is coated in crimson and flesh. It falls from his fingers, crashing to the ground. Wasting no time, his glistening hands unclasp her ankle restraints. She is still on her side. Francesca's top leg falls to join her other on the floor.

Bringing her knees to her chest, she attempts to curl into herself in a fetal position, wallowing in a puddle of her own blood, tears, and drool.

Her blonde hair is now stained a bright beautiful red.

Regardless, E would say she looks pathetic. Her true self is showing just before death strikes.

I would have to agree.
You don't betray your family.

CHAPTER 21

ELIJAH

I love watching people die.

By my hands or their own.

Lately, forcing people to end their own lives has been my 'kink,' as Rain would say. She also insists that curb stomping is another.

It's not that.

As my boot hits the back of a person's head, I breathe out as my body relaxes into it. The skull and bones cracking put me into a trance as the blood splatters around me. Seeing tiny white Chiclets against the dark floor or concrete stimulates my mind. The contrast is art.

When I forced my mother to walk backward into the fire, she did it. She didn't fight back or attempt to save herself. She just fucking did it. That fascinated me.

It made me wonder if others were the same. I've been curious ever since.

Typically, those I kill plead, beg, and cry for mercy. They try to bargain with me. It never works because I couldn't give a fuck. But it's me who kills them each time. Never have I given them the gun and said, 'shoot yourself,' until my mother.

With each step backward, she knew it was coming. The flames would engulf her, melting her skin and burning her alive.

She didn't move out of the way, she kept going until she tripped backward into the bright orange flame.

I still hear her screams, if the memory ever comes to mind. The distinct smell of her flesh filling the cave. I was satisfied. I was excited. My mind and eyes were captivated by it all.

And I've wanted to do it again ever since.

When we walked in here tonight, I got an idea.

Her endgame. Francesca.

It was planned in my head before we ever entered this room. Envisioning it as we walked up the stairs. As the Duke's and Duchesses watched us from the balcony, their entertainment for the evening.

Rain places my rabbit mask over my head, leaving it on my forehead so as not to cover my face yet. Her chain is still in my hand, I never let it go as I removed the grater from the diseased cunt.

As a child, I never liked Francesca.

I never liked anyone, and I still don't outside of Rain and my dad. But she is a particular breed that irritates me to no end. She's always begged for attention. This was just another one of those situations. And unfortunately for her, I was the one to give it to her.

Her dad—my uncle—is my dad's younger brother. He is a Lord, just like me. As my dad is the oldest, he assumed the position of Duke for our family. Which will be passed down to me one day. And I'll make sure my little bat joins me. Then, after us, the line will die. The rabbit will be retired and a new family will be inducted in.

Rubbing the cool metal between my fingers, I take in the sight before me once more. My little bat did so fucking good. Rogers must have been the one responsible for setting this room up, along with my dad. The choke pear for her was the perfect addition alongside the other antiques she likes.

"Should we leave it in or take it out?" My gaze wanders up her body. Bare legs, the white high-waisted skirt, to the white tight crop top, and her dark hair which is perfectly chaotic. Her makeup is smudged, screaming that she's been freshly fucked. But I couldn't give a shit. It only marks my claim more if people could see her without the mask.

Her eyes look up to the ceiling as she thinks, her teeth biting her bottom lip. "I want to keep it. Memories of tonight." I nod and turn my attention back to Francesca.

Placing my hand on the top of her head, I apply pressure to keep it still as I grip the key of the choke pear. Not bothering to turn it backward, I decide to pull it out of her mouth as it is, fully open.

"Last chance. Join The Exiled by marrying a Commoner and becoming one by default. Keep your filthy mouth shut and fall into place. You will never be a Lady despite your bloodline. Simply a Commoner, who once we are done with, you will be disposed of. Not even your own father gives a shit about what we are doing with you right fucking now. Your role would be simple. As a whore who spreads her legs plenty now, you would simply continue doing it with a gag in your mouth. But since my little bat has broken your jaw, perhaps the gag won't be necessary anymore."

Unable to respond, I take that as a no to my final offer and yank on the choke pear. The metal hits the back of her teeth, it rings heavenly in my ears. I pull again, and this time I hear a few cracks. Then once more. The choke pear comes flying out. My own momentum nearly knocks me backward. Her front teeth are chipped along with her canines and a few on the bottom. The familiar sound of screams and pain follow, no longer muffled.

Passing the pear to Rain, I say, "Leave it here, Rogers will collect it for you."

Walking the short distance, she places it on the shelf, then asks, "Can we keep all the others? I never got a chance to try them out." Her voice is cute and sad all at once.

"Yes."

Her hands clap together, excited. Turning around, her eyes are wide with the biggest smile on her face.

Racing over to me, she leaps into my lap and starts kissing my cheeks and lips in quick succession.

I can hear her nose scraping along the mask's edge before, breathlessly, she whispers against my skin, "Thank you."

This is the only state she should ever be in—happy.

Looking over her shoulder, I take in the sorry excuse of a woman on the floor.

"You wanted attention. Here it is. Now it's time for your final performance."

Fucking traitor.

CHAPTER 22

ELIJAH

Pulling Francesca up by her hair, more cries follow.

Should have shoved the grater down her throat and destroyed her vocal cords while I was at it.

Missed opportunity.

Because Jesus fucking Christ, she is getting on my last fucking nerve.

Her blood stained white-blonde hair is tangled between my fingers, the sight makes me sick. Only one female's hair that should be here is Rain's, while on her knees, choking on my cock.

"I know what you're thinking. And later," she says, bopping my nose then wrapping her arm around mine, and continues, "I'm glad you're back. I was worried. Feeling helpless. Not sure how to make it better. I hated it." Her face falls into my body as she holds me tighter.

It's an all too familiar feeling. It's exactly how I feel when she's sad.

"I'll never disappear like that again, I swear it, little bat," I reassure her, kissing the top of her head. It's something I've come to notice she likes. Head and forehead kisses, they always make her smile while her shoulders fall into relaxation.

"Let's finish taking care of this bitch and go home," I say, whispering into the crown of her head. I can feel her nod against me as she begins to let go of me. Her eyes pierce into mine. "I'll grab your bat."

I wink, so she pushes my shoulder, and I lower my mask over my face. The chain jingles as she bends over, picking the wooden bat up between her fingers. Looking up at me, she smirks. Her entire demeanor has changed, she seems relaxed for the first time since we landed in Montana.

Pulling on my cousin's hair, I drag her body behind me as I walk to the door.

Rain pulls her own mask down before I open it. The moment I crack it open even an inch, the loud music begins shaking the room, which is soundproof. The house is still dim, but voices are louder as more people must have arrived.

Stepping out, the Duke's and Duchesses are no longer standing against the balcony and the aerial artists have since vacated their ribbons. A few Commoners are up here, leaning against the wall, hiding from the main room's commotion.

Reaching the ledge, I drop the bitch. Her head bounces against the wood floor beautifully. Gripping the iron railing, I lean over and reach for the red ribbon left hanging.

As I grip the soft silk between my fingers, I pull it back with me and my feet meet the floor once more. Holding it out next to me, Rain grabs hold of it.

I sit Francesca up, leaning against the bars. Her head falls to the side, and her eyes are barely staying open, as more blood drains from her. If we don't do this now, we will lose her before I even get to finish.

Should have shot her with adrenaline, but fuck it, let's do this.

Taking the ribbon back, I toss it around my cousin's neck. Unable to pull her forward without her falling, I work quickly. I end up completing the noose knot on her front side.

Looking at Rain, I make eye contact with her, then point to the decorative table against the adjacent wall. Leaving my bat, she rushes over and pulls it over to me.

I scoop Francesca up from under her arms, then throw her on the table. I hop up on it next, and the legs shake as I stand on the top of the surface, bringing my cousin to stand with me.

My arm reaches under her, gripping around her chest while I hold her against me in order to keep her on her feet. My other hand rotates the ribbon so the noose knot is toward me, at the back of her neck.

Placing my lips next to here ear, I shout, ensuring she

hears every fucking word, "If you don't place your feet on the ledge, I will do it for you. Either way, you are dying here tonight."

She is lethargic.

Goddammit.

Quickly, I move my hands to her waist, hoisting her up so her feet touch the iron rail. The moment I let go, she's dead.

Looking off to the side, my eyes wander to the main floor. A couple familiar faces are standing, watching and waiting.

"Look, your dad's down there watching."

The last vision she will see. Her own father doesn't even want to help her. Proving to her everything I have fucking said.

"Do it. Fucking coward," I command, seeing if she has anything left inside of her to move forward. The weight of her is still relying on me.

This dumb bitch is on my last nerve.

Declining her birthright and being needy, relying on others until the very end.

She was given a choice. She didn't pick the right one.

Now it's time for her to face the consequences. She was warned.

Music is pounding. The floor on the second-story balcony vibrates beneath our feet as we stand on the table.

I yell once more, "Jump!"

A whimper leaves her mouth, Francesca's body

shaking with fear. Fear which she put inside of herself. It didn't have to be this way.

My mouth grazes her ear, the last words she will ever hear. "No one will miss you anyways."

A loud scream leaves her as my hands let go. Her final breath of oxygen enters her lungs.

Feet that were balancing on the wooden banister only moments ago are now floating in the air as she falls forward. The final seconds of her life are gone in a flash.

The silky red fabric that hangs from the ceiling dances. My eyes are captivated by it.

"Fucking beautiful, isn't it?"

The loud snap is music to my ears as gravity pulls her body down. The red aerial ribbon stays in place, creating tension. Opposing forces. The neck breaks. Her head falls to the side with her broken jaw hanging loose. Francesca's hair is soaked and colored red. The torn sweatpants dangle at her feet, her pussy exposed and dripping blood.

Our initiation as Lady and Lord is complete.

Rain looks over the railing, her eyes examining the hanging body. Others below are doing the same, as loud clapping follows.

Rain's head turns rapidly toward it.

Francesca's dad, my uncle Gregory, is cheering.

Rain then turns to face me, her eyes squinting as she points to him. My little bat is displeased. We can't have that, can we?

CHAPTER 23

RAIN

Her own father is clapping.

Reminds me of mine.

Flashes of my cleansing invade my mind. They are clear, vivid images. How he cupped me. Had his friends watch as I lay in the copper tub. Then how I prepared for him later, where he had me on that table ready for the taking. He just stood back and watched. He was going to let it happen. Until Elijah Sinclair saved me. Freed me. Owned me.

Where did that get my father? Dead.

Francesca's father is no better.

I watch as she dangles before us. Feet pointed to the ground, exposed and mutilated. She was going to ruin my family. She had to go.

Him.

He has betrayed his blood. He doesn't deserve to live another minute.

I wonder if E feels the same.

He hated his mom. She betrayed him terribly. Never picking him first. My poor boy.

Thankfully, his dad isn't like our past experiences. Nathaniel is like my mom. My eyes go bright while my lips curl, smiling. I wish she were here to experience this. They would have gotten along wonderfully.

But, instead, she's here in spirit. Always.

E jumps off the table and walks over to me. He raises his mask, exposing his face, then raises mine as he grips the back of my head and smashes his lips into mine. His teeth nip at me as he devours everything I give him. My hands grip his shirt, needing him closer to me. Our tongues battle for dominance as they become intertwined with one another. My nose is pressed tightly against his face, and I use his lungs for oxygen, breathing in through my mouth as we continue to kiss. E's lashes tickle me, and a chill tingles up my spine as I rise to my tiptoes. Our breathing gets heavy, and his cock strains against his pants as he grinds his hips into me. Opening my eyes, they look up to his. They are already open looking at me.

I've never done this, kissed with open eyes like this. But it feels more intimate, seeing into each other's souls during our battle of passion.

His grip against my head weakens, and his mouth

pulls back as I lean in. The tip of my nose rubs against his before settling back down on my feet. We still keep eye contact as he mouths silently, "Don't worry."

We both lower the black masks again over our exposed faces.

His hand gently touches mine, rubbing my palm in slow circles as he looks around the space, plotting. The movements abruptly stop. E knows exactly what he's going to do. I smile under my mask in delight.

He leads the way as he begins walking toward the staircase. I scurry after him, not wanting to be left behind, completely forgetting I couldn't as my leash is still in his hand.

Casually, he steps down each stair. I hold on to the cool railing against my hand, not wanting to trip, as the dim lighting makes it hard to see while stepping down each black step.

Reaching the main floor, we walk hand in hand toward his uncle Gregory, his dad, and a few others.

A bright light coming from beside me catches my attention. It's quick. As the door opens and then closes, it's gone. All that remains is that girl with the latex mask, but this time she is naked with only the mask left on. Something catches her eye. I follow where she is focused, and once I see where she is looking, I'm shocked.

Nathaniel Sinclair.

A glint of light catches his eye and I can see him looking back at her.

Shifting my eyes between the two, I watch to see who makes the first move.

The girl in the latex does. She steps away from where she is standing and walks away from the main room, disappearing down a dark hall. Nate catches me watching. His eyes widen through the holes in his mask. I bring my finger to my lips, zipping them closed and pretending to throw away the key. His shoulders relax. As we both focus back on E and his uncle, who are speaking.

It doesn't seem as if anyone else noticed Nate and I, all attention is on the two men before us.

E shouts over the loud music, "I can barely fucking hear you, old man," while motioning toward the outside.

Uncle Gregory steps forward and motions, *after you.*

We lead the way, with me and E still hand in hand, walking through the commotion of sweaty bodies, clouds of smoke and endless piles of drugs and booze. Those already initiated seem to be treating this as a party or rave of sorts. I feel claustrophobic. My chest races as my eyes squeeze shut. I need to get out of here. E can sense my distress. His casual walk has turned into brisk steps. He has reached back, nudging me to go ahead of him. As I do, he engulfs me in his arms, protecting me from outside factors.

Reaching the end of the room, we are standing in front of the beautiful, large windows. The moon is bright, reflecting off the river below. This property is stunning.

E reaches out, turning the glass door handle, and

pushes it open. The fresh air washes over us, and I close my eyes briefly as I breathe it in. The smell of nature invades me. My body relaxes, feeling peaceful again.

I step into the wooden deck which branches off to the side of the house, then up the stairs to a larger deck space.

The space is empty. Just the three of us.

Lounge sets and outdoor living furniture decorate the area, along with space heaters. This must be one of many outdoor spaces, as there isn't any sign of its use.

I presume we are going to take a seat and begin to walk toward the plush outdoor couch, but my body is pulled in the opposite direction, compliments of my leash. It nips at my fresh clit piercing which stings. A hiss sneaks out between my teeth.

Spinning around, I see we are headed to the ledge.

A breeze passes by, and the leaves in the trees rustle. The sound of moving water catches my attention. I find it soothing. My eyes are captivated by it, watching the current move it. The stars shine bright alongside the moon. I look toward E, curious if we can raise our masks. He still has his own on, so I leave mine as well.

"Nephew, you did well this evening," his uncle states as he comes to stand next to me, looking out into the distance. His cologne is strong, I scrunch my face at the smell. I hate it. It is overwhelmingly musky, in the worst way.

We don't acknowledge his statement.

E's cheek presses against the side of my head, his lips

whispering in my ear, so only I can hear, "Let's see if he can fly, little bat."

I want to smile with glee. Clap my hands at the excitement. As below us, the river is shallow with sharp mountain rock lining the edges.

Gregory turns to face E, who is standing behind me still. His back leans casually against the deck railing. His hands are in his trouser pockets as he crosses one foot over the other.

"Come on then. What did you want to discuss, nephew?"

In response, E's foot rises, bending slightly at the knee, before shooting back out and connecting with his uncle's abdomen.

He is caught completely off guard. As his body tips backward, his hands reach out of his pockets and his arms circle, looking for balance, which they never find.

With raised feet, he falls back. Loud hollers echo around us.

Lifting my mask, I look back at E, who has his own in his hand. My brows rise as the largest smile adorns my face. "Thank you."

He shakes his head at me in response. His dark, floppy hair hangs over his forehead as the skeleton face tattoo looks exquisite in the night light. The look on his face responds back to me, *don't be silly, I live for this shit.*

My brow furrows as I realize, "E, shouldn't there have been a splash?"

He tilts his head, his face concentrated. Nothing. No splash, no moans of pain. It's too quiet.

We both hold on to the railing and lean over, looking for the dead body. Scanning the river, nothing is floating, nor are there traces of blood. Moving to the rocks, they are clean of any debris.

An evil laugh erupts from E's mouth as he points down directly below us. Neither of us could have seen this happening with the darkness encompassing us.

His uncle didn't make it to the river or the rocks.

A broken-off thick, sharp tree branch sticking up from the earth has impaled itself through Gregory's chest. His body hangs limp in the air.

I join in laughing.

What a fucking night!

Then I realize, he sort of died similarly as my own evil father. The difference is that I stabbed the sharp dagger into his chest many times. Whereas nature stabbed Gregory for us.

I don't think it's a coincidence.

This all happened how it was supposed to.

Leaning back down, we begin walking toward the house. E pulls his phone out, his fingers moving quickly. Not even thirty seconds later, it vibrates.

I peek over to see who he is texting, not because I don't trust him, but because I am absolutely nosey.

> If you want to say goodbye, best do it before the cleanup crew arrives.

DAD

> *eye roll emoji*

I laugh at his dad's reply. I love their relationship.

Sliding his phone back into his pants pocket, E blows out a deep breath.

"Let's go home, little bat."

CHAPTER 24

ELIJAH

Standing in front of the large window, looking out into the backyard, a delicate blanket of white frost has settled on the yard and bare trees. Winter is arriving. The ground is only going to get harder, making disposals more time-consuming. Looking to the tree line, I know where I'll be spending my afternoon now.

A couple of days have passed since Hell Fire Night. The town has resumed normal business. Not a soul would be able to tell anything ever happened. All evidence was cleaned up before sunrise.

On the drive home, Rain was exhausted. Passed out the moment her body hit the passenger seat. I was still on a high, so when my dad called as we drove through town, I couldn't say no.

Looters were spotted at one of our fronts, an outdoor sporting goods store. Only fucking idiots would loot something The Exiled owned. I told him I would check it out.

By the time I got there, only one remained. With my car and headlights off, I waited. His head poked out of the smashed window, looking around for any witnesses before stepping through the debris back onto the sidewalk. His arms were full of shit.

Starting the engine, it roared to life as the lights shined brightly on his shocked face. He immediately took off in the opposite direction.

My car is faster. I pulled in front of him. Caught by surprise, he fell on top of the hood. All the shit in his hands flew everywhere and Rain slept through it.

Getting out, I found the fucker on the ground, crying. Next to him was a package of rock-climbing rope. Picking it up, I got an idea. As I opened it, I saw he picked the good shit, as it came with carabiners. Smiling to myself, I walked over to the rear of my car. I opened the trunk, threw the one end in, and then closed it shut.

The other end, I wrapped around his throat a couple times, shortening the rope's length, then knotted it. All while my foot was pressing his face down. Muffles of *"I'm sorry. I didn't know,"* followed.

When will they learn? I don't fucking care.

Lastly, I hooked the carabiner through his stretched earlobe for extra precaution because I wasn't going to lose him.

Stepping back, my boot was imprinted on his face. He looked much better this way. Then I went back into my car, slammed on the gas, cranked the wheel, and sped out of there. Smoke came from the tires as they spun on the road. A loud scream of terror followed as we took off. Looking in my rearview mirror, a sense of pride overtook me as I looked at the fuck trailing behind.

Once home, I didn't wake Rain immediately, instead checking on my new friend.

His clothes were torn to shreds, and exposed skin covered in road burn, including his feet as it appeared his shoes got lost at some point. The carabiner remained perfectly in place through his ear. The rope was frayed slightly but withheld the trip well.

Satisfied that he was still alive, I stepped over him.

As I did, something grabbed my ankle, and I looked down in disgust. How fucking dare he touch me? I kicked him off, then spat on his wounded body. "Don't fucking touch me."

As he rolled over, that was when I saw it. Half of his face was completely gone. Skin, brows, and lips were all taken by the road.

I was glad I hooked the rope to his other ear. Fuck me.

Leaving him to rot, I got my little bat from the car and carried her into bed.

That was two days ago, and I haven't checked on him since.

Thanks to him, I know what my afternoon will

entail. I have no choice, it's only going to get colder and the ground will become harder.

A small hand touches my back. I don't startle. I felt her enter the room, she's been watching me for a couple minutes.

She likes doing that. She finds me *'interesting.'*

"I have something to show you," I say, turning around and taking her hand. Rain is in my hoodie, which is hanging below her knees, with long fuzzy socks on.

She's perfect.

Walking through the main room, she follows without hesitation. I take her through the hall and stop before the secured door. With her hand still in mine, I move it up toward the scanner pad and place her thumb over the top.

Once scanned, the green light flashes and the door clicks open. Her face is shocked but she's also smiling.

"Only us. No one else. I told you that."

Biting her lip, she covers her mouth with her hand, trying to hide any emotion.

"But seeing it is different than just hearing it, E. Thank you," she says, as emotion appears in her eyes. Why is she sad over this? Shouldn't she be happy?

This time, she reads me before the words leave my lips. "They are happy tears, I promise."

Pushing the door farther open, I flick the light switch and walk down the stairs. Rain follows. No words are spoken as we make our way down, just the sound of our feet hitting each step filling the narrow stairwell.

As we get to the bottom, the strangest feeling washes over me. Similar to when I kill. Excitement, perhaps?

I stand to the side and let her go in front of me.

The loudest gasp leaves her, this time with both hands over her mouth as she turns to me in disbelief.

"E. Did you do this?"

I nod once in response.

Her focus moves back to the space, and she steps in slowly, with apprehension. Soft whispers follow, "I can't believe this."

As she reaches it, her hand slips from the sleeve and touches the cool surface. She looks back at me once more. "It's beautiful."

"Open it," I encourage as I stay back and watch her.

Her fingers slide to the handle, gripping it and then pulling open the pink steel cabinet door. As it opens, her face drops again.

On the shelves are familiar items, such as her choke pear from that night, in a glass case, along with a new one next to it. Another grater dildo, thumbscrews, iron pliers from the 1800s, and a matching pair of nut cutters. Metal hay and ice hooks, and this wild fucker called a heretics fork—it straps around a person's neck with the fork ends digging into the base of their throat at the collarbone and under their chin. The method for this one is sleep deprivation. They have to stay awake, and the moment they fall asleep? Dead. I also made sure the claw device Greta gifted me was in there too. Hanging on one of the doors she hasn't opened yet, because I got her two cabinets, is a spiked rabbit. When I found it online, I knew she had to have it.

Then a question I never expected leaves her, "When you were a kid... Did you ever try to fit in, mimic people, study their reactions?"

The fuck?

"Absolutely not. I couldn't give two shits about anyone or anything outside of me, you, and my dad. Understood?" I explain, stepping farther into the room.

Her fingers lightly brush against all her new toys. She doesn't look at me as she continues, "Okay. I was just curious. I've been reading up on psychopaths more lately. Just to better understand you, not ever to change you."

My head tilts sideways. "Why?"

Her face falls, the energy has changed. "Since that day, in the bedroom. I just want to be prepared... In case it happens again." She stops speaking, like there's a question it could happen again.

"Never again. I promise, little bat. Never. Not toward you or around you," I reassure her.

Her face turns toward me, her eyes soft. "I know. I believe you."

The loud ringtone of my phone breaks our moment. Pulling it out, I see it's my dad.

I answer, putting it on speakerphone.

"I need you both to come over," my dad says.

Rain smiles. "Hi, Nate, we will be right over." Her tone is excited once more.

Chicks are fucking weird.

Before my dad can respond, I hang up. They can chitchat in a couple minutes in person.

Rain steps before me. Her fingers dance along the stubble along my jawline, reiterating what she just said, "I believe you."

CHAPTER 25

RAIN

We are in the golf cart pulling up to Nate's and I am still shocked.

"And you didn't even wake me up? What if I wanted to watch?" I say to E, irritated. As we drove past his car outside, that's when I saw *him*, laying there frozen.

I'm pissed.

I've never seen a person be dragged behind a car before.

E side-eyes me. "I wake you, you're annoyed. I don't wake you, you're annoyed. What did your little research say about psychopaths around this?"

I know he's making fun of me now.

"Obviously, you wouldn't know to wake me. You

pick up on my cues. I get annoyed when woken up," I say, rolling my eyes.

His arms spread wide, as if to say, *see*.

"Did you know freezing to death is apparently one of the more painful ways to go? It starts with the fingertips, toes, nose, and ears. Which are the worst parts. Once it reaches your internal organs, it's like nothing. But the initial start of it, apparently hell," he throws back at me.

I laugh sarcastically, "Oh, doing your own research now?"

As we park, he looks over at me. "Obviously. I've had a guy attached to my car in the cold for two days. Skin scraped off with muscles and nerves exposed, I was curious."

And when will the dead man be leaving our driveway?" I ask.

A loud groan leaves him as he throws his head back. "I'll be in the woods after this, sorting him out."

His annoyance brings a smile to my face.

Getting out of the cart, we walk up to the large door and let ourselves in. E continues walking farther into the home he grew up in.

I wonder if his room is still here, unchanged. Or did Nate turn it into something like parents do once the kids leave the nest?

I glance up to the second floor. E must have noticed I wasn't behind him. "What are you looking at?"

With my head still lifted, my eyes shift to E. "Was your room up there?" I say with curiosity.

Walking back over to me, he replies, "Uh, yeah."

He doesn't get it. A childhood room is sacred. The memories and the innocence, all possibly preserved upstairs. Perhaps not so innocent in his case. Regardless, there is something priceless about getting to relive those precious memories.

"Can I see it?" I take a deep breath in as I ask, because I'm nervous he won't want to. His shoulders shrug, then he begins going up the large, grand staircase, hollering back, "You coming?"

Rushing behind, he leads me up, and instead of going across the second-floor balcony, we turn down the hallway. The cream walls are lined with thick, dark chocolate wood trim which matches the border of the flooring, which frames the cream carpet. A few rooms line the hall. The shine of the sun peeks through each doorway, except for one. The same one we stop in front of. I notice his breathing picks up, becoming more loud as he exhales through his nose. My hand touches his back gently. "We don't have to do this."

Shaking me off, he says, "No, it's fine."

His hand reaches the dark, circular metal knob, and it creeks as he turns it. The latch clicks, and the hinges creek the same way. Like no one has been in here since he left ten years ago.

The blinds are closed, so no sun shines in this room. It's dark as we step in. E flicks the light switch, and my sneezes follow.

Completely untouched.

The dome light shines down on the space. Thick dust covers the wooden shelves with matching furniture. Along with anything else it could latch itself onto.

His twin bed is against the same wall as the window, the bedding is black which matches the wooden frame. Two hand-drawn pictures by a small child are the only things decorating the walls. On white paper, done in crayon, a stick-figure boy with his bat standing alongside his stick-figure dad. Next to them, a stick-figure woman in a triangle dress lays headless on the ground. Toward the edge of the paper, the head rests with X's for eyes.

His mom.

Another one has black scribbles on it. I'm unsure of the meaning, but today is not the day to ask. This must be overwhelming to E, which worries me as dealing with emotions such as his own can be difficult.

I walk across the once cream carpet, which now looks like a filthy brown, to the shelves. One book is on it. As I touch the delicate leather binding, I realize it's a photo album. The laminate pages tickle my fingers as I drag them along the top of it. "Can we take this?"

E clears his throat. As I peer over, I see him standing at his bed. "Yeah, I will have Rogers bring it over." His tone is stoic.

"I slept here each night since I was five, with my bat next to me. Even during the night, I never let it go. My dad never made me feel different. He embraced my dark-ness." He pauses briefly before continuing, "My mom was a fucking mess. Their room was across the bridge, that's what I called it when I was little. But she always made a point to come stand outside of my door when she felt like screaming at my dad about me. *'The boy isn't normal. We should be sending him away, not encouraging this madness. He is no son of mine!'* were a few of the things she would say while doped up on pills. I always hated her. But I knew when I was ten, I had to leave with her. It was my last chance to experience shit outside of Bozeman before having to come back. It's what led me to you, little bat."

A single tear runs down my cheek to my chin, then drops onto my sneaker.

His head turns, looking over to me. "Don't cry for me, little bat. I'm not. She got what she deserved. I just had to play the long game." The corner of his lip lifts, his teeth playing with his lip ring mindlessly.

"Rain. Elijah," Nate yells from somewhere in the house. We both look in the direction of the voice, then back to each other. E makes the first move, flicking the switch and returning the room back to its dark state. I follow behind, stepping into the hallway and allowing him to close the door.

He shouts back, "Coming," as we move down the hall and back down the stairs. As we do, I swear from the corner of my eye, I see a tiny frame with long, black hair disappearing into another room. I look again, but no one's there and I can't hear anything.

Perhaps my eyes are playing tricks on me.

We make our way downstairs and find ourselves in

Nate's familiar office, which smells of leather, cigars and vanilla. Sitting on the brown leather couch, I curl my legs into myself then cover them with my oversized sweater. E sits next to me, leaned back and his legs spread.

Nate is sitting behind his desk. This is the first time I have seen him so casual, wearing an army green Henley with gray sweatpants. His signature glasses are missing and his hair is disheveled as he rakes his tattooed fingers through it, moving the stray pieces off his face.

That's when it occurs to me, Bozeman gets cold, Bozeman gets gray sweatpants season. I hide my smirk behind my sweater neckline. Acting like I'm cold, warming myself up.

Nate doesn't bring up E's bedroom. He has always been good about not pushing him.

"You both did exceedingly well during Hell Fire Night. The Duke's and Duchesses were most impressed with your display of your party favor at the end. And your uncle won't be missed, rest assured. With that, Elijah, you will be my right hand now. You are truly the only one I can trust in this organization. I'm not sure if you are aware, there is rumour that our King was taken out the other night as well. Change in leadership is upon us. I've been assured nothing will change for our family. Now that you have returned, our family officially over-sees the discipline and removal of garbage. While still keeping the police and judges under my portfolio. And Rain will be your right hand. The three of us need to stick together during this time of transition within the organization." He pauses, rubbing his hand over his face while letting out a deep sigh. "People do funny things to get ahead. We will need to handle those appropriately. Opportunists will not be tolerated. Loyalty speaks volumes."

Leaning forward, E clasps his hands together. "Understood."

The familiar sound of a phone vibrating catches my attention as it rumbles on top of the wood desk. Nate looks down, squinting at the small print, then laughs, "Fucking Delacroix. The man is wound as tight as the noose Francesca had wrapped around her neck." Then he continues to chuckle to himself.

E whispers in my ear, "They went to Harvard Law together, have known each other for more years than I have been alive. He is one of the few people my dad has around that I can actually fucking tolerate. He was likely the one in the warthog mask that we almost hit the night of Hell Fire."

I nod in understanding as a wave of overwhelming thoughts rushes through me. There is so much more to this than I can even comprehend. But I will have to. I am a fucking Sinclair. It's my duty. My eyes remain focused ahead as I watch Nate type a quick reply back. His gaze returns to us as he places his hands firmly on the wooden desk and stands. "Very good. Now you two go—rest. Oh, and maybe you can deal with the body still attached to your car? Things could get very busy for us soon."

* * *

It's later in the evening, the sun has set and a chill creeps throughout the house. One being from North Carolina, I am not familiar with.

E has been outside digging a grave for the majority of the day in the forest behind our house. He did it all by hand, which I thought was insane. Why get a digger machine? He said that was for the lazy. Who am I to argue?

At one point, I saw him walking back there with a head in one hand and legs in the other. I think he cut the guy up in the garage, as I didn't hear any commotion in the house. And he wasn't wearing any sort of bio suit, so I hope he burned the clothes after.

Sitting in the white tub with gold claw feet, bubbles cover my body up to my chin and the scent of lavender fills my nose. My head rests against the porcelain ledge. As the water becomes lukewarm, I lean up, turning the antique brass faucet. Hot, steamy water flows out of the tap, warming me up. Once satisfied, I turn it off and lay back down, closing my eyes as I relax. My mind for the first time in days is quiet. Or almost. One thing is floating around, but it doesn't revolve around fear or worry. I can feel the bathroom door open as cool air drifts in.

Exhaling a deep breath, I turn my head and open my eyes. E is leaning against the bathroom countertop, wearing gray fucking sweatpants. My mouth waters as I nip my lip. The most sultry voice I've heard comes from me. "Come here."

His laugh sends shivers all the way down my spine and directly to my pussy.

Sitting up, I move to the side of the tub, resting my arms atop it while leaning forward. He makes me wait, not moving. He likes when I beg. And beg I will.

"Please," I say, while batting my lashes at him.

Stepping forward on bare feet, his hands slide into his pockets. His tone is casual, when he says, "Good girl, little bat. Now pull my pants down, take what you want."

Reaching up, my wet hands drip down his front. I watch as the water droplets make his sweatpants darker around his already erect cock. Inching his waistband down slowly to build the tension and anticipation, I spot something new on his pelvis. *Rain Sinclair* is tattooed in cursive. It looks fresh. When did he do this?

"Keep going. I don't like waiting." E tsks me.

Continuing, I lower his pants more. His hard cock springs out, nearly hitting my face. His piercing has beads of precum on it. Reaching forward with my tongue, I lick the cool metal that goes through his swollen head. Lifting his shirt, he places it between his teeth to hold it up. E's stomach contracts as I go in once more, this time licking the slit. As his eyes hood, I go in for more. Craving every drop that he will gift me.

Wrapping my hands around his base, I take all of him inside of me. Gagging as I take him deep, sucking him hard as saliva drips out of my mouth. My tongue moves along the underside of his cock while I hollow my cheeks. He is huge, and I have always struggled to get him entirely down my throat. Breathing through my nose as often as I can, I work him, contracting my throat as he rubs against it.

A sharp hiss leaves him.

My baby E likes it.

Pulling him out, I catch my breath then take the tip of my tongue and brush it along the thick vein under him as slowly as I possibly can. His pelvis bucks forward as I lick his slit, then wrap my lips around his sensitive head. The metal from his piercing is cool against my tongue. I continue to tease, circling his tip as I watch his stomach contract once more.

He is using all his restraint to not take control.

Removing my grip, I brace my hands on his firm ass while looking up, and softly tell him, "Do it."

With permission given, he shows no mercy.

Gripping my hair between his fingers, he thrusts hard inside my mouth. Using me to chase his pleasure, and I fucking love it.

His movements become more rapid. Louder grunts begin as his ass flexes in my hands.

"Such a good fucking girl. Taking my cock. Letting me fuck your pretty little face."

My pussy drips at his words as my own breathing becomes heavier.

"Don't you fucking stop. You can take it, little bat.

Take it!" His voice has gone deeper, more raspy the harder he fucks my mouth. He pushes his shaft all the way down my throat, taking him the deepest I've ever had him. His pelvis slams against my mouth a couple times before he pulls out. My lips swell, and I wish I wore lipstick to mark him and have that added to his tattoo collection.

"Next time." The words come out softly from his lips before instructing me, "Mouth open, tongue out."

I obey.

With one last jerk of his cock, ropes of his warm cum begin shooting out of his tip, landing on my face as he paints me with it.

With hooded eyes, his lips murmur while taking me in, "So fucking beautiful."

More release coats me, some landing on my lips as my taste buds patiently wait for their serving of the salty white glaze.

A whimper leaves me, I'm desperate for it.

E's strong hand cups my cheek as he aims his cock at my tongue, allowing the last bit of release to shoot out, giving me exactly what I have been craving, and it's fucking delicious. As the final drop drips into my mouth, I lap it up and lick my lips, enjoying every moment of his salty orgasm that I own.

Letting go, he steps back and tucks himself back into his pants. I don't clean my face off, letting his sticky release dry onto my skin.

His beautiful blue eyes with the brown specks stay

on me as he praises me, "My little bat is a sinner with those moves."

His comment makes me laugh. Nervously, I respond with a slight hesitation, "We both are, E."

He looks at me inquisitively. "Do we need to go to church, grace the altar with our presence, and fuck our sins out of each other, little bat? Right before the priest. Perhaps bathe in some holy water while you sit on my face. As the good priest recites prayers over our naked bodies."

My heart is racing as I spit the words out, "I'm pregnant."

EPILOGUE

RAIN

Weeks.

It's been weeks since I dropped the bomb on E.

Based on when I had my period last, I'm easily eight weeks along.

I thought it was stress and all the changes that caused my period to run behind. Then my boobs started to hurt, which was unusual. My stomach was slightly more bloated than normal. Again, not having flown or been at this altitude, I thought nothing of it. My mouth was always parched. No matter how much water I drank, nothing helped.

Then it occurred to me.

With all the commotion of the past few months,

apparently my birth control wasn't always at the fore-front of my mind. But E's cock was, often.

Unable to sneak out without alarming my extremely over-the-top possessive baby daddy, I had to message the only person I know, his dad, Nate.

He had Rogers get a variety of feminine products, including tampons, pads, and a couple Diva cups. Mixed in at the bottom of the bag were a few different brands of pregnancy tests. This way if E was a nosey Nelly, he would be put off by the period products.

Thankfully, with his new project of *burying a dead body in the forest behind our house*, he was far too busy to care about a delivery.

Even with E outside, I still raced to the bathroom and locked the door behind me. Dumping everything out on the floor, I picked through everything, only taking the tests out.

I took six in quick succession. All off the same stream. I could hear my heart beating in my ears after each one.

I didn't get off the toilet while the timer was counting on my phone. I was frozen with anxiety.

Once the time was up, I still didn't move.

What if it's positive and we have a boy? E would be so fucking jealous of another man taking my attention, regardless of blood. What if we have a girl? Would E accept her? Would he even show an interest in her?

My mind raced and taunted me with *what-ifs* until my legs went numb from sitting for so long.

After standing up and cleaning myself off, I looked down at the counter where all six white sticks sat. And all six had positive indicators.

My heart sank. Fuck, how was I supposed to tell E?

Later that day, before I told E about the baby, he promised he would never react again like he did those days prior with his episode. He fucking promised and I was about to hold him to it, but then he surprised me with my pink cabinets full of fun goodies and his dad called wanting to meet, which put my announcement on the back burner for the time.

Before going over, I wanted to message Nate. Let him know what the results were, to ask him for advice on how to tell his son. Fuck, to even ask for advice for myself. This is when I could really use my mom.

Then, seeing Nate in his office, not pushing E by bringing up his room, I knew it was exactly how I had to handle delivering the news. Tell him, then let it sit. But first, I wanted to give him the best blowjob of his life, which I did.

After I told him, he stood before me in silence. He didn't move, nor did he speak. His gaze focused on the wall behind me, only blinking when he remembered to. Then he turned around and left.

Most people would be pissed at this reaction. But I wasn't. This was better than his violent outbursts. I will take his silence over that any day. And just like Nate, I wasn't going to push him.

That night, I didn't see him. I also didn't go looking.

I went to bed alone and I was completely okay with that. After waking up the next day, I strolled, still half asleep into the kitchen and began making coffee.

"Something is up with my dad. I sat watching his house all night. He had someone over." I nearly jumped out of my skin, not expecting E to be in here. Turning around, I see he is lying on the couch with his legs crossed. His eyes looked tired and his hair was a mess.

I acted surprised. "Oh?"

"Yeah. I couldn't get a good look at her as she drove by, but I did notice she had long black hair. I sent the plate number to my guy, I'm waiting to hear back. I'll have her entire background before lunch."

I closed my eyes softly and took a deep inhale, held it in, then exhaled.

"Okay. I'm excited to hear what you find out."

His poor, fucking father.

The day rolled on as normal and then carried into the next. I hadn't heard more about his super spy mission, but I presumed it was still active as he was missing from bed for a second night. But at least he was speaking.

Then today happened.

I'm leaning over the large kitchen island, drinking a hot cup of green tea. Rogers just brought over the photo albums from E's old bedroom. I am about to start looking through them when the man himself comes bursting in through the front door, slamming it hard behind him.

As he walks past me to the back door, over his

shoulder is a dark circular fence post, maybe four feet long. In his other hand, a sledgehammer.

"Um, E... What are you doing?" I ask curiously.

"Pigs." His response is quick as he continues to move through the house. My eyes widen in shock, unsure what to make of his statement.

Taking a sip of tea, I continue with a follow-up question, "What pigs?"

"We have six coming in, in a couple hours and I need to build their fence," he tells me as he stops before the back door, turning around.

"Well, okay. Have fun." I try to sound as excited as I can without offending him with my confusion, knowing he is clearly still in a very fragile state.

This continues for an hour, with him going through the house with more posts and chicken wire fencing.

On his last trip through, all he had was a nail gun. I decide I am done asking questions for the day. But he decides to shed some light on the situation himself. "I read that babies are needy little assholes. That thing growing in you for the next however long would prefer to know both parents, if possible. So, pigs. They will help dispose of the bodies when it arrives. Thus, *it* will know both of us. But I will never hide who I am from *it*. If *it* should ask what pigs eat, I will say bodies. I also read they can be a lot of fucking work. Do you know how often they shit? So yes, pigs. They will help free up some of my time to help."

My eyes want to cry from happiness. My mouth

wants to laugh at the insanity of this entire declaration. But most of all, my heart wants to burst from how much I love this fucking man.

Pigs.

I can tell we aren't fully comfortable with the news yet, it seems. But he is speaking, he is building, and he is planning for the future with fucking pigs.

"Did you know you can grow mushrooms off people?"

His comment throws me off guard. Is my poor baby E having a nervous breakdown? Are we becoming mushroom farmers?

"You will never guess who my dad keeps having over."

My interest is piqued. "Well, don't leave me hanging!" I say eagerly. I've also been dying to know. I think it's the same person I saw there last time we were over, it has to be.

"Greta's granddaughter."

My mouth drops in shock. I have so many questions. Greta was married? She has kids and grandbabies? I've met the woman once and became instantly fascinated.

Before any words can escape me, E continues, "I have plans, little bat. Big fucking plans. If he is going to be parading that girl around the grounds of the house and think I wouldn't notice, he is in for a shock when I am this block's fucking welcoming committee!"

The End.

WHAT'S NEXT?

I am absolutely obsessed with the Sinclair family, and I
hope you are too!

Because ***Unholy*** is coming next. Are you ready to get to
know Nathaniel Sinclair?

If you want a sneak peak into his life, check out

Phantasm by Harleigh Beck

Nathaniel and Delacroix's bromance is next level!

Special **THANK YOU** to Ms. Harleigh Beck for letting
our words crossover. I absolutely adore you!!

-Kins

ABOUT THE AUTHOR

Kinsley is a Canadian, Dark Romance Author who dabbles in Taboo, Forbidden and is currently in her Horror Era. When she isn't plotting her next twisted book or watching true crime docs with her cats, you can find her working for the man. Reading. Or drinking wine while causing chaos with friends, let's not limit ourselves now. Make sure you follow Kins on her socials and sign up for her newsletter to see what is coming next!

authorkinsleykincaid.com

ALSO BY KINSLEY

FORBIDDEN

Let's Play

Within the Shadows

Lessons from the Depraved

Haunted by the Devil; The Devil's Society

Sinner; The Devil's Society

Homecoming; The Devil's Society

Unholy; The Devil's Society - 2025

TABOO

Wrecked

Sutton Asylum

Dark Temptation: Part One

Ghost Dick; A Port Canyon Chronicle

Dark Temptation: Part Two

Lessons; An Extremely Fucking Taboo Extended Epilogue

Brothers Bond

Sick Obsession - Coming Winter 2024

Fuck Me, Daddy; A Port Canyon Chronicle - TBD

Taboo can be found via the authors' website.